BLACK RAVEN INN

BOOK II IN TARYN'S CAMERA

REBECCA PATRICK-HOWARD

For Ruby Cravens, who gave me a picture of Elvis and said, "You'd better have that out someplace where I can see it when I come visit you"

and

Emma Jane Chumbley, who gave me a copy of Gram Parsons' "Grievous Angel" and Emmylou Harris' "Duets" and said, "You'd better actually listen to them."

CONTENTS

PROLOGUE

Sleep meant certain death. If there was one thing he'd learned, it was that.

He was heavy eyed, and lethargic. The jumbled thoughts in his head were all over the place, as rowdy and insistent as any child he'd known. As he sank back into the standard motel room pillow, however, his body began to change.

Warmth started at his feet and traveled throughout his body in calming waves, moving inch-by-inch all the way to his ringing ears and into his brain where his mind finally quietened and settled. The euphoria that followed had him smiling and flinging out his arms, the Messiah on the cross. His stomach moved up and down in shallow motions as his breathing became heavier, more labored.

The torment he'd been living with was gone; his problems dissolved into the air, scattered away by the ceiling fan above. He could do anything, *be* anyone...

Everything was going to be okay.

His head nodded back and forth in a familiar rhythm, crushing the pillow below. Was it one of *his* songs or someone else's?

Well, it didn't matter.

Beneath him, he could feel the firmness of the bed and slippery material of the generic quilt. He was touching them, yet both felt so very far away. Perhaps they belonged to someone else, or to another time period. He couldn't be sure. He might as well be floating on a cloud.

Gratitude for the respite swelled in his chest so he closed his eyes and gave in to the sensation, the feeling of being *outside* his own body. The aching in his heart and the pains that regularly plagued his body began fading, replaced by a sense of relief.

His eyes shot open almost at once. "No!" In a blind panic he struggled to focus on an object in the room, anything to bring his attention back to reality.

He must *not* fall asleep. He wouldn't.

His eyes scanned the room in alarm until they landed on something familiar. With an audible sigh of relief, he fixated on his guitar case propped up by the door. Beaten and covered in chipped paint, it was comforting to see the old case standing there like a sentinel. Or a friend.

For a brief moment, his head cleared. The pain returned with a vigor, but he was no longer swimming in the murky, dangerous waters. Maybe he needed a doctor. Something wasn't right. He'd taken the same amount he always did. He was careful not to take more, just enough to make him human again. But he'd been around the block enough to know that something was wrong.

He wasn't feeling sick, exactly; in fact, he'd never felt better. His mind was comfortably numb, his muscles loose and languid. He even felt a tinge of excitement about the new album and tour and God knew he hadn't been able to feel that particular emotion since he was a little boy. The world was beginning to make sense again.

If he could just keep his frigging eyes open.

There was a dim throbbing sensation in his stomach but this he could ignore. It was just a nuisance, really. Probably his poor old liver. He'd given the old girl a workout, for sure. He was going to cut down on some things as soon as this tour started. *She'd* see to that. She always did.

The drowsiness struck him again, this time even harder. He wasn't sure he could fight it. Again, he felt his eyes closing, the weights on his eyelids lowering them like a bucket in a well. Try as he might, he could not pry them open, not even when he rubbed furiously at eyelids with his black-stained fingers.

They felt so good closed, though. The second they were shut the pain disappeared and he was transported to another world, one in which he soared straight through the roof of the grungy motel room, where his friends and mother awaited him with open arms, where his body floated with weightlessness, free from the worry and restraints of the world below.

Maybe just for a second, he thought with contentment. *Just a minute or two wouldn't hurt. I'll wake myself up...*

He'd been on the road for weeks, after all, and in the studio nonstop for nearly seventy-two hours. He could use a little rest.

Though he was already lying down, he soon felt himself falling backwards and as he descended, an ethereal angel appeared before him. Her beautiful chestnut hair swirled around her lovely aristocratic neck and cascaded down her back; her bright blue eyes shone with heat. The silky dress she wore was covered in tiny roses and he knew without touching it that would be soft under his hands, just like her skin would be. He groaned aloud when she reached her hands out to him and smiled, the radiance stemming from her body brighter than the white light surrounding her. Without shame, a tear slid down his cheek as their fingertips touched.

He continued to plunge backwards, falling into a depth that swallowed him whole.

6

ONE

Taryn *didn't just read* the email from Ruby Jane Morgan multiple times–she printed it out (on cardstock, no less) and hung it on the refrigerator. She was still trying to decide whether or not framing it would be a little much, a little *too* cheesy.

"Eh, what the heck?" She grinned with pride as she stood back and studied it. It wasn't like she had tons of visitors over at her apartment to laugh at her corniness.

So, until she could find a frame worthy of it, the short but incredibly important message from her childhood idol hung in the middle of her ancient refrigerator, held up by a magnet from Daytona Beach. When she *did* frame it, she'd attempt to do it in the most tasteful way possible. Not cheap, plastic, fake wood but maybe a nice silver frame. Something from a real department store, not just the discount places where she usually shopped.

She'd had the email for three weeks now but that didn't matter. Taryn was still experiencing the afterglow, similar the all-consuming elation she'd felt after attending an intimate Rosanne Cash concert at the Exit In when she was twenty-three. After that concert she'd replayed every note, relived each blessed moment, and thought of little else after the show ended.

And *that* afterglow had only lasted for a week.

"Ruby Jane Morgan," Taryn had gushed to Matt, her best friend and sometimes boyfriend, over the phone. "Can you believe it?"

In excitement she'd forwarded him the email, the one propositioning her for a job, as soon as she'd received it.

"Well, she's just a person, right?" he'd asked, mystified at her reaction.

Taryn gasped. She thought she felt her heart skip a beat. "'Just' a person? Ruby Jane is *not* 'just' a person. She's considered one of country music's biggest legends. And she's still alive which, you know, is kind of a big deal with legends. She's right up there with Dolly and Loretta."

"Who's Loretta?" Matt asked innocently.

"Oh, you did *not* just say that."

"I just don't think I know who she is," Matt said lamely.

Taryn felt an unreasonable irritation at his lack of enthusiasm over her exciting and unexpected news. She wasn't sure how such a person had even known who she, multi-media artist Taryn Magill, even was. It wasn't like she was the toast of the art world, though some wouldn't even consider her a real artist, considering her subject matter.

"She's done harmony on almost every important country album for the past forty years. Created an entirely unique sound that people from every genre use? Been inducted into both the Country Music Hall of Fame *and* the Rock and Roll Hall of Fame? She's inspired multiple generations of artists, won five Grammys?" Taryn offered helpfully.

"What's her famous songs?" Matt asked. "I probably know them."

Taryn appreciated the fact that, in spite of his obvious lack of interest, he was still trying to play along but his question left her feeling deflated.

"Well, she's never really had a *hit*. She's more of an artist than a hit maker. But there was 'Crying a River' and 'Remember December' and 'Angry at the Moon'? I mean, those songs didn't go to number one or anything but they still get played on the radio and a lot of other people covered them."

"Don't think I've heard of them..."

Taryn exhaled and shook her head in disgust at her camera, Miss Dixie, who watched her from across the room. She was almost certain that Miss Dixie smiled back at her in sympathy.

"Well, and then there's Parker Brown." When Matt didn't respond, Taryn forged ahead. "When he was still alive they recorded a lot together. 'Watch Over Me in the Night' is considered a gospel standard, even though technically it's about needing drugs. Bet they'd love *that* in church if someone in the congregation ever figured out the lyrics. And '1,000 Roads' was on at least three movie soundtracks in the 1990's alone..."

"Parker who? I'm sorry. I just don't know her," Matt apologized. "But if you're happy about it then I am excited for *you*."

"Some people have zero appreciation for country music history or tradition," Taryn grunted, feigning agitation.

Realizing the conversation was completely one sided, Taryn changed the subject. She later hung up trying to remind herself that she wasn't exactly interested in everything that *Matt* was into, either.

Like end-of-the-world apocalyptic movies. ("The Day After" had given her nightmares for weeks; she still couldn't hear the phrase "nuclear winter" without having a mild panic attack.)

Or space stuff and avocados.

Eating at restaurants and then returning home and trying to recreate the dishes they'd just had so that they never had to go back again.

And definitely not anything related to math, which seemed to rock *his* world.

It was okay that they were two different people, with different interests. What mattered was that they loved each other and, even more, that they were *friends*.

Still, she thought it would've been nice to have someone who shared her enthusiasm of being contacted for a job by one of the most famous, and important, women in music.

Now, as Taryn dropped onto the wilting, but still cozy, featherbed that had once belonged to her grandmother, she let her mind wander.

Whether Matt appreciated it or not, she, Nashville native/artist/photographer and sometimes ghost hunter Taryn Magill, had just been commissioned to create not one, but *four* paintings of the Black Raven Inn—one of Nashville's oldest, and most notorious, motels.

And she'd been hired by someone she'd grown up listening to so much that, to Taryn at least, Ruby Jane Morgan felt like more of a family member (distant cousin perhaps) than a celebrity she'd only met through recordings.

"I don't care if nobody else understands," Taryn whispered to her ceiling. "This is one of the most exciting things that has ever happened to me."

Ruby Jane Morgan's music had been there through so much of Taryn's life that it was impossible to think of a past without her. Her music was *that* important to Taryn.

And later, when she'd lost her fiancé in the fiery crash, she'd felt Ruby Jane's own personal tragedy coming through in her music and that, too, had meant something to Taryn.

In fact, on the long dark nights when Taryn had thought there was no longer a point in going on, Ruby's music had saved her.

As a child she'd literally worn the 8-track version of Ruby Jane's concept album out. The album (when listened to in chronological order) told a story about a woman who lived during the Civil War and dressed as a man to fight alongside her husband.

She'd played it so much that her parents had dreaded going anywhere with her because it meant getting in the car where the album played on a continuous loop. In fact, Taryn wasn't convinced that they didn't have something to do with the mysterious disappearance of said 8-track.

"Sorry, honey," her mother had apologized one hot August morning, they'd all piled in and Taryn had recoiled in surprise as the Rolling Stones spilled from the speakers. "It must have fallen out. Or something."

But her mother had not sounded apologetic at all and, in fact, her father had even looked a trifle relieved. And guilty.

Luckily, however, her grandmother had bought her a new version, this time a '45 record.

"Keep this here at *my* house," she'd winked as she handed it to Taryn on her next visit. "We'll take special care of it here and I can guarantee you it won't go missing."

Taryn had listened to it every time she visited, and played it out later when she moved in. Eventually, her grandmother Stella had replaced it with a CD, doing it quietly without making a fuss, as she did most things where Taryn's needs were concerned.

And now...

She was going to meet Ruby Jane. *In person*. Not as a fan, either, but as someone the artist herself had sought out. It was a dream come true–to be considered an equal, more or less, by your idol. She was meeting her on equal footing, under the impression that she'd somehow gained the other woman's respect.

"I knew that BA in Fine Arts would come in handy eventually," Taryn laughed gleefully, tossing a throw pillow in the air. "It only took $60,000 in student loans to get here!"

TARYN *FIGURED* she probably spent more time between the art supply store and camera repair shop than anywhere else when she wasn't out on the road. For the first time in a long time she would be working a job right there in Nashville, her hometown. That made things much easier; she knew where everything was and could run out to the store and pick things up whenever she wanted.

Still, it was important to get a head start. "I need to hit the ground running with this one," she told the salesman at the camera store as she picked up an extra battery charger for Miss Dixie.

At least he'd had the courtesy to look impressed when she name-dropped her client.

"Ruby Jane Morgan?" he'd asked incredulously.

"I *know*, right?"

"What are you going to do?"

She quickly filled him in on the job and then watched as he processed the information. Finally, he narrowed his eyes and leaned in to her. "You know that place is meant to be haunted, right?"

Taryn nodded. She knew that paranormal investigators had gone in there and supposedly caught orbs and EVPs on recordings. She wasn't going to put too much stock into those until she explored it herself, though.

"I've heard that," she replied. "What do you think?"

"I don't know man," he said, scratching his head in thought. "Some pretty weird shit has gone down at that place, you know? Some bad characters hanging around."

"You think the place is haunted because of the people who stayed there? Kind of picked up on their energy?"

"Or maybe they were drawn there because it was a bad place," he reasoned.

Taryn bit her lip and considered. It was the chicken or the egg riddle.

"Well, good luck," he said sincerely. "Break a leg and all."

Luck was something she might actually be needing.

Taryn would be doing a series of paintings for the old Black Raven Inn, a special project commissioned by the entertainer herself. For the next couple of months, Taryn would be spending her days immersed in the history and atmosphere of the rundown, seedy roadside motel.

The Black Raven Inn was *not* the kind of place she was used to working at.

Granted, the structures she was usually called in to paint tended to be neglected, rundown, and even abandoned, but they'd all contained their own kind of unique beauty–or at least some fascinating historical significance that the community was intent on seeing preserved.

Not this time.

There was nothing pretty about the Black Raven Inn, nothing exciting ever happened there. At least, nothing that anyone was *proud* of. It was like the Viper Room in Los Angeles, which would always be known as the place where River Phoenix overdosed on cocaine and morphine. People drove by the old motel to point and whisper, but it wasn't a part of Nashville's history that the city boasted of in its brochure. It would never appear alongside, oh say, Belle Meade or Grassmere on a downtown billboard.

The Black Raven Inn was a far cry from the opulent splendor that was the Jekyll Island Club Hotel or even the fine-looking reckless beauty of Griffith Tavern. This was unlike any other place she'd ever worked.

For the most part, Taryn was hired to recreate buildings to reflect their glory days. She was brought on board to restore (on canvas anyway) the magnificence of old private residences, historical buildings central to the town's development, and other noteworthy structures that had, for various reasons, fallen into disrepair over the years.

She'd worked at antebellum mansions that had remained in the same family for eight generations. Quaint mills turned into charming B&Bs. Soaring courthouses built right after the Civil War. School houses constructed by the WPA in the Roosevelt era. Buildings with historical significance. *Sentimental* significance.

She'd been employed by historical societies, nonprofit organizations, private homeowners, and even concerned citizens who raised the money themselves through crowdfunding sites to hire her. On canvas, she could revision the building's past and recreate it through her paintings to reflect the grandeur of its heyday–before it lost a wing or a roof or most of its backend to a fire.

Sometimes her paintings were the *only* thing anyone had to visualize what the building had once looked like before it fell into ruin. Oftentimes, the buildings had been constructed before cameras were popularized, or even existed. Or, perhaps, the only pictures made of it had been lost over the years. They'd been destroyed by storms or fires...

Occasionally her paintings were given to architects for the sake of remodeling jobs, or her employers simply wanted them for the sake of preservation, especially if the building was on the verge of demolishment.

Now, for the first time *ever*, Taryn had no inkling as to why she was hired or for what purpose her work would be used.

"Nobody will miss the Black Raven Inn if someone just tore it down," she'd confessed to Matt. "Trust me."

Unlike some small hotels that were old and ugly but still held sentimental value to those who'd stayed there and treasured fond memories of the place, she highly doubted if the majority of the folks who'd stayed at the Black Raven Inn even *wanted* to remember their time in it. Or could.

"You should have read the reviews of it before it closed," she told Matt. "In fact, you can still read them. They're still online. Just don't do it before you go to bed."

"I think I'll pass," he'd replied drily.

"Your loss," she'd laughed. "You're missing out on some incredible reading. One reviewer called his review 'The Second Layer into the Fiery Pits of Motel Hell.' I mean, how awesome is *that*? And that's not even the worst one!"

She could feel Matt shuddering all the way from Florida. There were few things he hated more than the idea of dirty hotel rooms, bedbugs, and cockroaches.

Guests at the Black Raven Inn enjoyed all those and more.

The motel had turned off its "Vacancy" sign for one last time a year ago, but before it closed it was well-regarded as a seedy establishment that nobody with any sense visited after dark. It was a well-known fact in Nashville that the motel's parking lot and rooms were filled with hookers looking for quick cash and lonely men looking for a quick companion. Addicts looked for a quick fix, pushers for a quick sale. And down-on-their-luck entertainers who'd lost everything to hock and needed a place to crash before running home with their tails between their legs, full of stories of how they'd "almost" made the big time.

But while Taryn had trouble understanding *why* Ruby Jane wanted her to do the work, she had no trouble when it came to understanding why Ruby Jane *herself* had bought the old place (though the wild price of $1.3 million dollars threw her a little).

The motel was, after all, the scene of not only one of country music's most senseless tragedies (VH1 still counted it as one of the "top 10 heartbreaks in music history"), but the setting of a catalytic moment in Ruby Jane's own personal life.

Her musical partner and rumored lover had died in Room #5 nearly fifty years earlier, the result of an apparent overdose.

That monumental loss to the music world changed the way some record labels would handle the welfare of their entertainers on future tours, and Parker's memory would forever cast a shadow on each album Ruby Jane would go on to record—all thirty six of them.

If there was one thing Taryn understood, it was the inability to let go of someone who had died tragically and unexpectedly.

Especially when that person's death was your own fault.

"YOU'RE *NOT* going there alone, are you?" Matt asked in dismay.

"Uh, no?"

"Taryn!"

"What! It's not like someone is going to shoot me in broad daylight," she muttered as she navigated the busy street.

"You just spent the past two days telling me how awful the motel was, and I *did* read some of those reviews. They were as bad as you said they were," he admitted.

"Yeah, but that was when it was *open*," Taryn teased him. "It's closed now!"

"And I'm sure the abandonment has made it a dozen times better," Matt remarked wryly.

Taryn wasn't meeting with her new employer for another day but, as nervous as she was, she wanted to be as prepared as humanly possible. She'd stayed up most of the night before doing as much online historical research as she could and it had been eye opening.

Thank God for You Tube.

Never before had research on a site been so entertaining or enlightening (or well documented; most of it was like watching an episode of "Cops", indeed, an episode of "Cops" *had* been filmed there).

Today, she was going to visit it in person.

"It's not like I'm not prepared," Taryn promised Matt. "I've got my mace and pocket knife."

"You know they'd have to be right on top of you for that knife to be useful," Matt said.

"Yeah, well, that's what the mace is for!"

"I remember that motel when we were growing up. It was bad twenty years ago," Matt mused. "My parents used to talk about it in a whisper, even spelling the motel's name up until I was ten. Like 'raven' was a bad word."

"Maybe they thought the bad word was 'black'," Taryn snickered.

"Considering who we're talking about, you have a point." Matt sighed. "I refuse to believe I came from them. I *am* going to order that DNA test one day."

"I can see the Jerry Springer episode now... 'Help! I'm A Genius and My Parents are Morons: Who's My Daddy?'."

Matt laughed in spite of himself.

Having lived between Nashville and Franklin her whole life, Taryn also knew the Black Raven Inn; everyone did. Growing up, to Taryn and her classmates it was known as the cheap motel that singers who had zero money and fewer connections stayed in until they "made the big time." In college, it had garnered the reputation as a place *so* bad and *so* dangerous that cops no longer even responded to complaints. High school kids even pooled their money to stay in nicer places after school dances; it's cheap prices weren't worth it.

It advertised itself as a "no frills budget motel" but that was code for "crack house" around town.

"Did you notice that the motel's website said it had a 'vintage feel'?"

Taryn snorted. "Yeah. Saying it has a "vintage feel" and claiming it contains 'some of the original features and fixtures' might have sounded good and looked attractive on paper, but what it *really* meant was that the building hadn't been updated since it was built. Original features meant something totally different when one is talking about lighting fixtures versus toilet seats."

"I could never sit on a toilet in that motel," Matt said, his voice shuddering.

"I could never sit on a bed in that motel," Taryn agreed. "I hate to think of the things that went on there."

Unfortunately for its neighbors, it was located in what was turning into a desirable part of town. The area was becoming gentrified and the eyesore had everyone up in arms. Hipsters didn't like their upscale shops and fusion restaurants being just a stone's throw away from its run-down entrance.

The new condos and townhomes building up around it were currently on the market for half a million bucks for a 2-bedroom unit. Taryn still couldn't get over the idea of living in what basically constituted as an apartment for so much money. Especially considering that her job as a freelance artist had her traveling all over the country. It provided her with a glimpse of other markets and just how far a dollar could stretch.

Expensive townhomes and condos, boutique hotels, specialty coffee shops, bakeries with artisan bread, daycares that cost more than her college tuition ten years earlier, upmarket shops...

And the Black Raven Inn.

A blemish on the Nashville roadmap that stuck out like the oozing sore it was, making everyone who lived, worked, and played around it cringe in disgust.

Still, the property had two acres in a prime location. The sex shops and massage parlors that had once surrounded it had been bought out, closed, and razed.

Everyone on that side of town was hoping that once the hotel closed, the razing would come again, especially now that the property had been sold. When it *did* come down, and everyone assumed it would, Taryn was sure she'd hear an audible sigh of relief from all of East Nashville.

She had no idea what Ruby Jane's plans were for the unmentionable blot on the landscape. Most people weren't even aware that the singer was the one who'd purchased it; they assumed it was a corporation or real estate mogul who intended to develop it into some high rises or new chain hotel. Perhaps a nice Hibachi Grill, surrounded by trendy boutiques. Or a Whole Foods Market. Maybe an Embassy Suites with a manager's cocktail hour and made-to-order omelet bar.

Taryn had a feeling they were about to be sorely disappointed.

TWO

*T*he *Black Raven Inn* didn't look that bad from the outside. Well, it was *bad*, but it wasn't scary-bad. In fact, Taryn thought it was rather charming in a neglected, kitschy kind of way.

"Eh, I've seen worse," Taryn said as she shrugged her shoulders.

Despite the ominous name, the building was painted a cheerful yellow. Or rather, it *had* been a cheerful yellow a long time ago. Over the course of several decades the color had faded and was almost white in some places; in others it had peeled and flaked off, leaving behind crumbling scars of bleak concrete. As an old roadside motor lodge, it only had one floor and was the kind of the place where you could drive right up to your door. The windows, now boarded up to slow down the vandals if not stop them completely, still mostly contained the bright red shutters that flanked them.

The 1950's-era sign that still rose proudly above the building had once lit up the area at night, blazing stark neon colors across the sky.

It was miraculously still on, but only the letter "I" in "Inn" still worked. The other bulbs had either burned out or been intentionally damaged from people trying to *put* them out.

The parking lot and motel were surrounded by a makeshift plywood wall in an attempt to keep trespassers away. There was a gate, though, and Taryn squeezed through it easily enough.

Worried about people who shouldn't be there, she carried her "weapons" in her back pocket. Although, to be fair, if someone attacked her she'd never have a chance. It took her a solid minute to get the blade out (the fear of cutting herself was strong) and the one time she'd tried the mace she'd almost blinded herself.

Still, it was something.

Taryn didn't need to worry about people, though. She was the only one trespassing at the moment.

Up close, the motel didn't look so much different from some of the roadside inns she'd stayed at on job assignments. The income she earned from recreating the past with her paintbrush earned her just enough to pay the major bills and give her a little left over—it didn't exactly leave her living high on the hog.

Of course, things had changed over the past few months. The settlement she'd received on her last assignment on Jekyll Island had allowed her to live a very comfortable lifestyle and, if she continued to manage her finances prudently, she wouldn't have to worry about money for awhile. She couldn't quit working, of course, and would still have to take on jobs but she could select them more wisely now and not have to take everything that was thrown her way, like she had in the past.

"If I sold Aunt Sarah's house…" Taryn mumbled as she trudged across the parking lot.

But that wasn't a thought she seriously entertained. Sure, the old farm house in New Hampshire would fetch her a pretty penny if she put it on the market, and the attorney had assured her it would sell quickly, but Taryn couldn't stand the thought of parting with it, especially after having paid it a visit at the beginning of summer. It was going to take a ton of money to fix it, and she'd need all those grants and loans she'd researched if she was going to preserve it, but it was worth it.

"Maybe I'll even live in it," she mused thoughtfully, her tennis-shoed feet crushing weeds that poked up through the cracked asphalt.

Matt, though. *Matt* would be a problem.

He couldn't possibly leave his job at NASA and relocate to the woods of the northeast. He *said* he could, that he'd go wherever she went, but she wasn't sure she could take on that responsibility. What if he hated it? What if he got up there, after quitting his job, and grew depressed and ended up resenting her for taking him away from the one dream he'd had since childhood?

"What if I'm not really in love with him?" she asked herself out loud.

That, of course, was at the heart of the issue and something she struggled with every day.

Taryn had loved Matt since the day they'd met as children—two misfits who had bonded together and created a magical childhood fortress nobody else had ever been able to penetrate or share. Not even Andrew, her fiancé who'd passed away in the car crash that had changed her life.

And they had a tremendous amount of chemistry together. Not only could they read each other's thoughts from hundreds of miles away, but touching him was electric.

"But still." She sighed.

That niggling "still" was what kept her awake some nights.

If they were truly in love, wouldn't they have moved in together by now? Or made some kind of formal commitment? After all, they'd been in a physical relationship for a year. And although there had been talks here and there of the two of them moving in together or making a more central base together, the discussions were always vague.

"It's a fact. I've been spoiled by romantic books and movies," she groaned as she stood in the middle of the parking lot and stared at the building in front of her. "I've got to cut back on the Rom Coms. Kate Hudson and Sandy Bullock, we're going to have to break up for awhile."

She hoped they wouldn't miss her too much.

Maybe *this* was what love felt like in real life. Maybe it was more complicated and stickier than she'd originally thought as a young idealist engaged to Andrew. Back when she'd felt butterflies every day.

"I still feel butterflies," she said. And she did. In fact, she was feeling them right now, just looking at the Black Raven Inn. "I still get them."

Now, the butterflies came from somewhere else. She got them from the old houses and buildings she worked with. Taryn had never met an old house she didn't like. (Windwood Farm might have been stretching it, but to be

30

fair she liked the *house*. It was everything that went on inside of it that turned her off.)

THE *MOTEL* she stood before had seen better days for sure, but there was still something mesmerizing about it.

It was nothing compared to the sprawling, glossy complexes built today. The chains with their cookie-cutter rooms and lookalike lobbies. Interior designed to include the same generic prints above all the beds, the same duvets, and same marble backsplashes.

The high rises that climbed into the air with their state-of-the-art fitness centers (key card entry only, please) and pristine indoor swimming pools with WiFi access in every corner.

Televisions that allowed you to order room service without even picking up a phone.

Wake-up calls set by pushing a series of numbers.

Checkouts by leaving your key card in the room and agreeing to the receipt via email.

Why, these days, you could stay in a hotel without ever interacting with another human being.

The Black Raven Inn consisted of twenty rooms, all with kitchenettes. It had boasted a swimming pool but that had been filled in years before; local skateboarders had used it for practice and one had actually broken his neck. That had put an end to that bit of fun.

There were parking spots in front of each room, as well as about two dozen general spots. The doors were made of cut-rate wood, some with holes in the bottom where someone had given them a good kick or fallen drunkenly into them. The rooms had never upgraded to key cards; they still used the "old fashioned" keys in their rusted holes. Brass numbers hung, some lopsided, in the middle of each door. Most were tarnished from years of neglect and some were missing altogether.

"Souvenirs," Taryn laughed, the sound strangely hollow in the barren landscape. People would take just about anything if they could get their hands on it.

The main office's entrance was under an awning that allowed cars to drive up and stay covered while the owner checked in, was boarded up. Taryn couldn't see inside.

Someone, or more likely several people, had graffitied over the pavement by the entrance and over the boards that kept people out (hopefully kept them out and not *in*). Some of the images Taryn found fairly interesting—popular cartoon characters and three-dimensional graphic designs. These were interwoven with curses and would-be "Satanic" symbols like pentagrams and upside down crosses.

"Someone needs to do a little Googling." Taryn sighed, tracing her finger over a pentagram with the word "Satan" scrawled inside it.

With the complex enclosed inside the fence, Taryn felt cut off from the outside world. She didn't mind this.

Although she could hear the traffic speeding up and down the road less than one-hundred feet away, she couldn't *see* it. With her music playing as she worked, it would be easy enough to block out the sound. She'd been promised that although the fence would remain, the boards and all barriers to the interior of the motel would be removed. She'd have free access to whatever she needed.

Taryn continued to walk around the outside of the motel, occasionally pausing to step back and take it all in, or move in closer to touch a board on a window or a door knob.

When she reached Room #5, Parker Brown's room, she hesitated. It looked normal enough. It was just a door, after all.

Without warning, the sound of footsteps running down the pavement filled the air. There was an urgency in them, a force that had Taryn jumping and yelping. She turned, expecting to find a police officer or fellow trespasser coming towards her. Her hand immediately moved to her mace, just in case it was the latter. The sound was right on top of her.

There wasn't anyone there. Taryn was the only person in sight.

Wrapping her arms around her for comfort, she stepped away from the hotel, walking backwards while still keeping it in view. Her skin had grown cold and clammy, her face chilled from a breeze that didn't exist.

"Why is it so cold?" she asked herself. "The temperature around the motel has to be a good ten degrees colder than it is out here in the parking lot."

Taryn got a flash of darkness then, like a shadow that crept across her line of vision. It was thick and opaque and smelled of decay.

But there was nothing there.

"The motel's meant to be haunted," Taryn had told Matt when she forwarded him the email from Ruby. "But it's not like I haven't dealt with *that* before."

"I have to warn you," Ruby Jane had said in her email, "it's in terrible shape. It looks like a place that's either full of ghosts or should just be torn down."

Taryn smiled at the thought now, trying to shrug off what she'd just seen and felt. After all, Ruby's words and the camera shop's musings could pretty much sum up most of Taryn's favorite places.

THREE

Ruby Jane Morgan might have had multiple awards on her mantle, but from the outside her house looked like any other home one could find in any upscale subdivision. No towering gate with posted guard deterred autograph seekers. The circular driveway boasted a Prius (Taryn resisted the urge to peek in the windows) and a dirty blue Chevy truck. The side yard was fenced in and Taryn's presence was met by a melody of barking dogs as they clamored over one another to check her out.

The expansive front lawn with its ornamental bushes, landscaping stones, creeping vines, and greenhouse flowers had clearly been professionally designed but there were also toddler toys scattered around the manicured grass. An

36

electric pink Barbie car, big plastic slide, and a cheap inflatable wading pool with a sailboat floating upside down inside were basking in the autumn sunlight.

"Those are going to leave a mark," Taryn said, looking down at the grass that was already yellowing beneath the toys.

She was thrilled that her idol was only human.

Still, it was hard to imagine that the woman whose albums Taryn had collected since she was a kid was basically just a grandmother with yapping dogs and generic toys from a strip mall store.

Taryn tensely smoothed her tunic down and ran her tongue across her upper teeth again, eliminating wrinkles and lipstick stains. She had stressed over her outfit all morning. She wanted to appear professional without looking like she'd tried too hard. The best thing about working *this* job out of Nashville was that she had access to her entire wardrobe. She'd made use of it too, trying on everything she owned at least twice before settling on the skinny jeans, knee-high boots, white peasant tunic, and infinity scarf.

She wasn't sure what she expected, as she stood on the porch of the Tudor style home and rang the bell, but it certainly wasn't that the lady of the house herself would open the door. When Taryn found herself face to face with the star, she thought she might pass out.

"Hi!" Taryn said brightly instead, hoping her words would come out in the correct order. Her mouth was as dry as a desert. "I'm Taryn Magill. I'm a few minutes early but I wanted to make sure I'd find it and..."

She was talking too much and too fast. Ruby Jane, who stood barefoot in her foyer, holding the door open in welcome, smiled indulgently. She'd probably seen and heard worse.

"I know who you are," she said pleasantly when Taryn paused to catch a breath. "I saw your picture on the internet."

The thought of a celebrity kind of cyberstalking her sent Taryn reeling into a parallel universe. Now she thought she might throw up. Instead, she tried her best to smile wider. "I am *so* happy to meet you," she bubbled.

And, with that, she was invited inside.

SHE'D *BEEN* sitting across from Ruby Jane ("Call me 'Ruby'") for half an hour, and Taryn was only *just* starting to feel like the situation might actually be real. For the first few minutes she'd felt like she was watching a movie and that she, herself, was nothing but a minor character. The feel of the soft leather cushion on the couch beneath her, the steaming mug of tea warming her hand, and the sugar particles on her lips from the cookies she'd been offered and accepted were all real enough, though.

She's just a person, Taryn reminded herself. *I have to treat her as though she's just another paying client.*

In the meantime, she tried to ignore the big framed picture of Ruby goofing off with Willie Nelson that hung on the wall within her line of vision.

"I'm a big fan of your work," Taryn heard Ruby saying.

Taryn was sure she was hearing things. "Excuse me?"

"Your work, I'm a fan," Ruby said again with the patience of an angel.

The older woman who sat across from Taryn wore yoga pants over a sinewy build, a navy blue T-shirt, and had her hair pulled up in a sleek bun. Bright green polish decorated her toes and she wore horn-rimmed glasses. Except for some light pink lipstick, she didn't wear a bit of makeup. She appeared at least fifteen years younger than what she should've looked, yet it didn't seem to Taryn that Ruby'd had any major work done.

"You said that in your email and it surprised me," Taryn admitted as she placed her mug on a coaster. The last thing she wanted to do was leave a ring on the old maple coffee table. "Unless you're in the historical business, so to speak, most people have never heard of me. Or of what I do."

What Taryn *didn't* add was that she'd also gained notoriety in the paranormal world, especially after her stint at Griffith Tavern. She was still occasionally surprised to find her name pop up in supernatural forums whenever she ran Google searches on herself (not that Taryn actively Googled herself often, but she was only human).

"I'm on the board of several historical preservation societies," Ruby admitted, her speaking voice, unlike her singing voice, was gentle and soft. "You did some fine work on a painting of a house down in Alabama that I grew up coveting."

"I remember that house," Taryn recalled fondly. She'd been with Andrew then, and the house was an antebellum mansion. They'd fallen in love there. She'd never forget it. "It had the most beautiful ballroom."

And Andrew had seen a ghost in that ballroom, Taryn thought. She wouldn't forget that, either.

"I've looked at your online portfolio and you do incredible work," Ruby continued. "You capture such detail in your paintings. I feel as though I could walk right into them. I'm an amateur photographer myself and enjoy taking photos but what *you* possess is a real artist's soul."

Taryn preened under the attention, and it was all she could do not to turn the conversation back around to Ruby's career and gush in return. She didn't want to come across as a creeper fangirl, though. Best to hold off until Ruby actually liked her. (If that ever happened.)

"I'm going to need four prints in total," Ruby said. She bent forward and removed a sheet of paper from the coffee table between them. When she handed it to Taryn, she saw that it was a meticulous list of the required paintings and what Ruby sought from each one.

"As you can see, I'd like one of the courtyard, a wide angle landscape of the exterior encompassing as many of the rooms as you can get, the lobby, and the interior of one of the rooms."

Taryn nodded as she read over the specifications. Behind the list was a contract.

"I'll let you read over that," Ruby added. "It's standard. Says you won't use the prints for any other purposes, that you'll seek permission before using any reprints for advertising, and that you'll adhere to the schedule."

Taryn nodded again as she read. It was pretty standard, like most of the ones she signed.

"And there's a privacy clause at the bottom, too. It basically says that you won't publicly repeat anything I might disclose in confidence. That means no interviews with the press, no blog entries, etc."

Taryn tried to imagine a world in which Ruby Jane Morgan shared her deepest secrets with her over chocolate and brandy. It was an exciting thought, but unlikely to happen.

"Oh, and one more thing," Ruby added brightly, tapping her fingernails on the table. They, unlike her toenails, were not manicured. Instead, they were stubby, crooked, and caked with dirt–like she'd been digging in the garden.

Taryn paused in her reading and looked up, marking her place with her finger.

"If you take any photographs of the motel then I'd like to see them. Actually, I'd like copies if you don't mind. That's in the contract as well. I am going to provide you with an SD card for this job. If you can just meet with me on a weekly basis I'll transfer everything over to my computer..."

Ruby faltered then and glanced down at her hands. Taryn saw that the long, elegant fingers were now nervously twisting and pulling at themselves. There was a slight change in the air, a subtle elevation of energy. It didn't chill her but instead sent a wave of heat creeping up her back. She could feel beads of sweat balling under her lightweight scarf.

"That's no problem," Taryn replied. "I usually take a lot of pictures of the places where I work. My clients have never been interested in them before but taking the photos is one of my favorite parts of the project. I'd be glad to share them with you."

Ruby offered a thin smile and bobbed her head, the bun at the back moving up and down like a little ball. Taryn returned to her reading.

"I am sure people are curious as to why I've bought the old motel," Ruby offered distantly after a moment of silence.

Taryn wasn't sure if that was a tactic to see what she thought or if Ruby was just thinking out loud.

"Well, I grew up around here so I know about the motel, of course," Taryn said cautiously. "It's actually an excellent example of its kind. Run down, of course, but probably salvageable."

"I always thought it had a bit of a charm to it myself," Ruby admitted, raising her eyebrows. "Most structures like that have been razed in favor of modern developments."

"I think that's a shame," Taryn said and she meant it. It *was* a shame.

Both women were skirting around the fact that Ruby's former partner had overdosed on heroin and carted away from Room #5 in a body bag. And Taryn certainly wasn't going to bring it up. But, as it was, Room #5 was the white elephant hiding in the room.

Taryn wondered how long it would be before it was brought out and made to dance.

WITH *HER* boots kicked off and her sweaty feet propped up on the arm of the sofa, Taryn flipped through the television channels and tried to find something mind numbing to watch. She was a sucker for reality television of all kinds, and if that didn't work there was usually always some trashy true life movie on one of the women's channels. Nothing was satisfying her tonight, however.

She was anxious about her new assignment.

Ruby had been nothing but polite while still maintaining a professional distance, but Taryn couldn't ignore the project's brevity. Clearly, the motel was important to the singer, for reasons that she didn't have to share with Taryn, so that made this job more personal, and stressful, than most.

"Like the stress of working with someone famous wasn't enough as it was."

Taryn planned on starting the next morning. Miss Dixie, her beloved camera, watched her from the library table by the door leading into her short hallway. She looked pumped and expectant.

"Yeah, well, I'm glad you're ready for it," Taryn tossed her way.

She'd begin with the pictures. For the first few days, she'd walk around the motel and snap as she pleased, taking shots of the features that called to her.

Every building spoke to Taryn in a different way. Sometimes it was the windows that called to her. Sometimes it was the outside spaces—the porches, yards, patios, courtyards, and balconies. Other times it was the interior details like the carvings on the mantles, the gleaming natural wood panels or bannisters, or the ornate crown molding.

This was something she let Miss Dixie take the reins on, and Taryn never knew what would happen until her fingers began working and her camera started clicking. The two of them were a pair and worked as partners. She never went anywhere without her camera; Miss Dixie wasn't just a tool—she was Taryn's other set of eyes.

She was her friend.

After spending some time getting to know the building and taking dozens, if not hundreds, of pictures, she'd upload them and go through them one by one. It was from these shots that she'd start putting the painting together in her mind.

Only then, when she felt like she really knew what she was working with and could see the intricacies and nuances of the structure when she closed her eyes, would she begin working.

"I promise all the barricades will be removed by tomorrow morning," Ruby had promised her. "I've also hired a security guard. He won't get in your way but I don't want anything to happen to you while you're there alone. As an artist, I understand that you probably work as the mood strikes you. Aker is on standby, ready to go when you are. Just send him a text and give him a 30-minute warning. You all might want to work out some sort of schedule, of course."

"A security guard? Like a bodyguard?"

Ruby had laughed then, a tinkling sound that rang throughout the room, filling it like tiny bells. "Oh, it's not as bad as it sounds. Aker and I go way back. In fact, he probably remembers the motel the way it *was*. He's been around Nashville all his life."

While Taryn didn't relish the idea of someone possibly standing over her and babysitting her all day, she understood Ruby's position. If Taryn got hurt or someone tried to bother her, Ruby would have insurance issues on her hands, among other things.

It was the first time she'd ever had her own personal bodyguard. In some ways, she was moving up in the world.

Taryn had just settled into a television show she could live with when her phone rang. The ringtone played Coldplay's "The Scientist" (her own inside joke) and as soon as she said "hello" Matt went into a spiel about his day.

"My students are driving me insane," he groaned dramatically.

"You missed your calling as an actor," she retorted. "So much drama."

Matt had taken on student interns from a local university. He both loved the idea of acting as a mentor and struggled with the notion of being in charge of so many people at once and not having any peace and quiet. He was an introvert at heart and mostly preferred to work alone. They were alike in that respect.

"Are you going to dock their pay?" Taryn teased him, knowing full and well that it was an unpaid position.

"Maybe," he grumbled. "Or take away their access to the pop machine. A little less caffeine would do a few of them some good."

"That's just mean, Matt."

Taryn never went anywhere without a Coke, and a backup drink.

"So, tell me about your meeting," he said after going on a ten-minute rant about the lax work efforts of the younger generation. "How'd it go?"

"Weird," Taryn answered, putting the television on mute so she could talk. "I mean, Ruby was nice and friendly. Just as pretty in person as I imagined, if not more so, but it was still strange to be in the presence of someone like that. I am still pinching myself."

"So how do you feel about the job?"

Cold, wet fingers wrapped themselves around Taryn's feet and left them numb. The chilly sensation started at her toes and slowly slithered its way up her body, leaving patches of ice along the way, until it reached her scalp. The hairs on her head stood at attention, one by one. She shook the feeling off with a twist of her head, shivering.

"Okay," she replied at last. "I think it's going to be fun. And I hope she likes what I do."

"But? I hear a 'but' in there..."

"I don't think she *needs* me," Taryn said at last. She wasn't going to tell him about what she'd felt at the motel, not just yet anyway.

"There are hundreds of photos of that old place floating around," she said. "Google it and you'll find everything you need, including paintings people have already done over the years. She doesn't need *me* to show anyone what it looked like in its prime."

"Maybe she just *wants* you," Matt suggested. "Rich people are like that. They spend their money on weird stuff."

"Like old, trashy motels their friends committed suicide in?" Taryn suggested.

"Yeah, like that."

"Maybe..."

Taryn wasn't convinced. Ruby hired her for a particular reason, she was sure of that. Taryn wasn't psychic. She had her sensitivities, true, but she needed Miss Dixie for most of that work.

Still, she was talented at reading people and all her meters were going off with this project.

She was sure Ruby Jane was hiding something.

FOUR

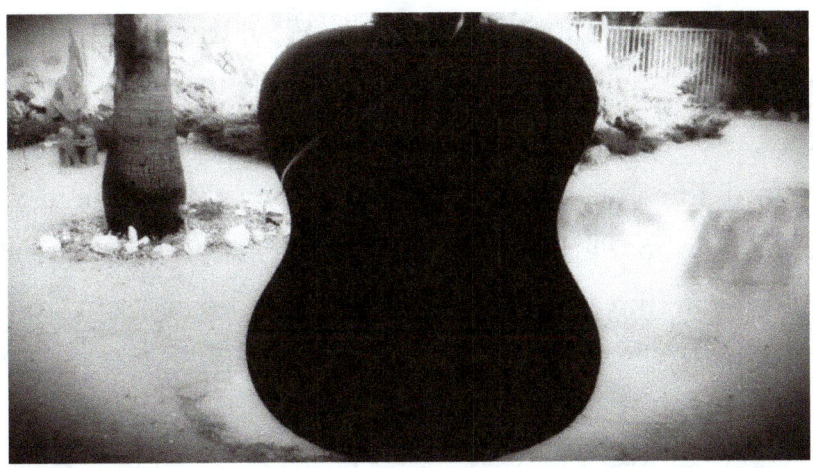

The sky was ominous for Taryn's first day of work at the Black Raven Inn. As she stepped out of her car and busied herself loading her various lenses into the camera bag, she felt the first fat drop of rain. It was cold on her back and had her shivering.

"Well, dang it."

Taryn stopped, held her breath, and waited. If the sky was going to open up then she didn't want to get anything else out and risk damaging it. None of the rain drop's cousins followed him however, so she exhaled and continued her task.

The red sedan parked next to her contained Aker, her security guard for the next couple of months. Aker was a retired police officer and former Marine. He was probably in his mid-sixties but looked forty. When she'd introduced herself and made a joke about finally being successful enough to have a bodyguard, he hadn't cracked a smile on his hard, lined face. In spite of the gloomy sky and menacing clouds he wore dark sunglasses. She wasn't entirely sure she could pick him out of a lineup if he turned out to be psychotic.

It was all very Hollywood.

"Wait just a minute," Aker barked when Taryn started towards the motel's front door.

He'd been in the middle of unfolding a chair for himself and now he sprinted towards the building, sticking his hand back to hold her off. "I need to re-check the interior and perimeter."

So Taryn stood in the middle of the empty parking lot, camera slung over her shoulder, and waited. She felt like she was on a crime show, waiting for the Swat team to give an "all clear."

The boards were gone and both she and Aker had a master key to all the doors, although he was the only one with one for the gate. Now she waited impatiently as he entered the building, long flashlight raised in his hand, and screened the handful of interior rooms that ran off the lobby. She waited again once he returned and surveyed the front of the building, looking for signs of break-ins and people who weren't supposed to be there.

"I'd say you're safe to go," he declared as he stalked back to her, arms crossed in front of his chest.

"Do we have to do this *every* time?" Taryn asked.

"Yes, ma'am," Aker replied, the clouds reflecting in his shades. "You never know who's going to be here that isn't meant to be."

Taryn offered a half-hearted "thanks" and then headed towards the entrance again, Aker's eyes boring into her back. When she neared the door she turned and looked back. He was busy setting up his folding chair again. She guessed he intended to camp out right there with her as long as she was working. It was a little weird but what could she do about it? She had worked in stranger situations.

At least it wasn't a gaggle of little old women, sitting in a row of lounge chairs sipping on martinis while they watched her paint the country club. (True story.)

The lobby door still had all its glass, which was more than could be said for the windows surrounding it, so Taryn opened it and stepped inside as though she were a guest checking in.

The "lobby" was a grotesque ghost town. It always surprised Taryn at how some empty buildings looked as though everyone just got up one day and walked out, leaving everything behind.

The Black Raven Inn's lobby was no exception. There were still papers on the desk, keys to most of the rooms dangling from hooks in the wall, and even outdated computer equipment hiding under multiple layers of dust.

Between the dark sky, awning, and the fact that there were only two windows to begin with, the room was so dim it was hard for Taryn to see anything. Soda cans and food wrappers littered the floor and she found herself treading over these gingerly, mindful of stepping in something she might not be able to get off her shoes later. Or *on* something that moved and squeaked.

The "lobby" was nothing more than a room big enough to hold three metal chairs, a desk she could barely see over the top of, a small table that held an ancient coffee maker and a coat rack.

Oddly enough, the coat rack still sported a dark-colored man's wool coat. It was impossible to tell if it was black or navy blue yet it hung there, neatly, among the disorder that surrounded it as though the original owner was still planning on returning for it.

The coat, waiting for someone who was never coming back, tugged at something in Taryn. She found it both incredibly sad and a little creepy. It was a sign that the world moved on, sometimes when life itself didn't.

Taryn turned Miss Dixie on and took a shot of the coat rack. The room suddenly lit up with artificial light, making it even spookier and sadder.

Ruby had told her that the electricity was working but when Taryn flipped the switch on the wall nothing happened. An empty bulb socket above her revealed the reason.

"I'll tell her about that," Taryn said loudly, her voice booming in the small, quiet space.

For now, she whipped out her cell phone and turned on the flashlight app to light her way.

A short hallway ran off from behind the desk and she followed it, now a little relieved that Aker had gone in before her and checked things out.

"He might come in handy after all," Taryn mumbled.

The first door she came to was closed and Taryn used her free hand to push it open. A collection of mops and brooms promptly greeted her—all of which threatened to tumble out and attack her in one fell swoop.

"Shit!" she cried as she juggled the cleaning equipment and her phone and attempted to corral them back into the tiny space. Apparently, Aker had either not checked that room or had stuffed everything back in the way he found it.

The second door was open about six inches. She gave this one a push with her foot, ready to tackle anything that might want to jump or fall out on her.

It was just a break room.

A large table with peeling Formica set in the middle of the room, taking up most of the space. There were coffee mugs on it, some of which looked to still contain dregs that had rotted over time.

The vibrations of her feet padding across the floor sent bugs scurrying out from every corner, frantically trying to make their escape as they ran every which way in panic, some scrambling on top of one another in their haste.

Taryn, who was not particularly squeamish but still not a fan of ugly bugs, jumped aside and did a little dance over the offending insects as they headed straight towards her and the open door to freedom.

The break room was gloomy but she supposed it had done the trick at one time. In addition to the table, nearly hidden under the garbage and even a few needles (she didn't want to think about *those*), there was a twin-sized bed pushed up against the wall. The mattress was lumpy, dirty, and sagged in the middle. Smeared across the middle was a big, dark stain. Blood maybe? Taryn didn't want to think about *that,* either.

Against the other side of the wall was a dated, brown, rusted refrigerator. "No way on God's green Earth," she muttered as she turned away from it. Nothing would have her opening it to see what kind of hell lived inside.

She'd just pretend it didn't exist.

"I have a feeling I'll be thinking that a lot about this place."

Still, Taryn had a job to do. She spent several minutes taking shots around the room, making sure to get the generic motivational nature posters, slightly discolored from the sunlight, dust, and cigarette smoke. She took pictures from several angles of the room using her wide-angle lens to get the space in its entirety. Then she turned to the windows and took shots of them from the bottom and sides.

Lastly, although she wouldn't use them for the paintings, she took pictures of the horrific mattress with its fear-provoking stain, the filthy table with its collection of unmentionables, and even a line of what *had* to be roaches marching in an orderly single file line to the door.

"Let's get one thing straight," Taryn declared, hand on hip. "I don't mind abandoned. In fact, I *like* it. I don't mind dingy. That has its own kind of charm. But I don't do nasty. And this is just *nasty.*"

She couldn't imagine Ruby Jane sauntering across the revolting floor in her expensive shoes, with the scent of decrepit neglect and what, to Taryn, smelled like the hint of feces, clinging to her willowy frame and beautiful hair.

But, hell. She didn't really know Ruby at all, no matter how many interviews she'd read or how often she listened to her albums. Taryn had to keep reminding herself that just because she grew up with Ruby's music didn't mean Ruby had grown up with *her*.

Maybe this *was* Ruby's kind of thing.

TARYN *SPENT* the rest of the dreary morning wandering around the motel's boundaries.

She snapped pictures of the doors, interior courtyard (all the rooms had back doors that opened up to a common outdoor area, complete with fire pit and picnic tables), and whatever outside furniture was left behind and not hauled off by looters.

Aker always kept his eyes on her when she was within his vision; she could feel them watching, even though she had her back to him and he pretended to flip through a stack of magazines he'd stacked neatly on a cooler by his feet.

"You okay over there?" she called out once.

He'd grunted in response and waved her off with a meaty right hand.

It was clear to Taryn that he could care less about her; he was simply hired by someone with a lot of money and his job was to keep *that* client happy and satisfied. Taryn was a necessary evil.

She briefly wondered what he kept inside that cooler of his. Surely not beer. He appeared to take his job far too seriously for that. Mineral water? Nah, not manly enough. Probably some kind of protein drink that came in a powder pack he had to mix up. Something with the picture of an iron fist on the packaging. Or a snake.

By noon the sky was black and Taryn could see the lightning flashes to the west. There was a terrible storm coming and she was about to be in the middle of it. The lighting was getting bad already; she might as well pack it in for the evening. It would take an extensive amount of editing on what she'd already taken to make them presentable. That wasn't something Taryn would normally worry about, but now that she knew Ruby wanted copies, the pressure of quality fell upon her.

Still, even as she felt the first few experimental raindrops fall lightly on her frizzy head, she found herself stopping in front of Room #5.

The tarnished brass room number had come unhinged by a screw and dangled upside down. The doorknob had been brass at some point, but years of grubby hands had faded it and rubbed off some of the finishing. The once bright blue door was dingy and dirty, streaked with mud and what looked to Taryn like feces. The door had been kicked in at the bottom, the wood splintered and scruffy.

Someone had taken a black spray paint can and written "Peace" at the top. Only they'd apparently ran out of paint there at the end so it really read "Peac." Someone else had attempted to draw a red heart inside a neon green guitar around the room number but the green paint, over the blue, got lost. The color reminded Taryn of bile, the kind she saw when she'd been vomiting for awhile and had nothing left in her stomach but acid.

To the right of the room was a window. With the plywood barrier removed, she was able to see the glass, boldly intact. The tattered lace curtains that hung limply inside were surprisingly feminine for such a place; the holes in the fabric looked like they'd been made by cigarettes and moths.

As she gazed at their delicateness in a sea of hostility and deterioration, she thought she saw one of them flutter, a slight movement that had her catching her breath a little.

"Closer," a voice whispered provokingly. "*Please.*"

Casting a quick glance over her shoulder, she looked back at Aker. He was in his chair, a book in his hand. He could have been reading or napping; it was hard to tell behind those dark sunglasses. He didn't appear to be watching her, though.

He certainly hadn't whispered to her.

Taryn reached her hand out towards the door, fingers trembling a little. When her fingers touched the cold, hard knob, an electric jolt flashed through her. The blue spark that shot out from the door flashed in front of her just as a fat raindrop landed on her nose. Both had Taryn jumping back onto the sidewalk, clutching Miss Dixie for comfort.

"Oh, come on," she laughed nervously. "It's just static from the weather."

Yet from the corner of her eye, she saw the hint of movement in the window again; the curtains *were* moving. It wasn't her imagination.

And she hadn't imagined the voice. Something was inside that room.

Taryn stood as still as she could and watched the door and window. *He* had died on the other side of that wall, Ruby Jane's band mate and, by most accounts, her lover. A heroin overdose.

When the motel was still open and operating, musicians and devotees had flocked to the room and made a virtual shrine of it, leaving behind guitar picks and song lyrics they'd composed themselves in honor of his untimely death.

Many claimed his ghost still lived in the small room, forever trapped within the four inauspicious walls.

Taryn would have to go inside sooner or later. Her curiosity would eventually get the best of her, not to mention the fact that Ruby had specifically asked for a painting of the interior.

She'd save the exploration for another day, however. If Parker Brown's ghost was indeed living within Room #5, then she'd meet him eventually.

She always did.

FIVE

"So what's the verdict, doc?"

Taryn had been waiting on the examination table for thirty minutes. Her doctor always ran late, but since she usually had a book with her she didn't normally mind. However, today the sky was clear for the first time in four days and she was itching to get back to the motel.

She'd wanted to reschedule the appointment. This was an important visit, though, and she needed to be there.

Her doctor, a young woman with long brown hair, closed the door and pulled her stool up next to Taryn. In her hands she held a folder, several inches thick. It was Taryn's records from the past year. She'd turned into their biggest client; Taryn liked to think her insurance payments were keeping the entire office up and running. She'd been there so much that the staff had gotten together and bought her a Christmas present the year before.

"It's not *great* news," Dr. Culver warned her.

"Ruh roh," Taryn grimaced. "Did it grow?"

"Yes," her doctor admitted. "You started out at 3.8 and now we're up to 4.2."

For those with Ehlers-Danlos Syndrome, the aortic aneurysm was the development nobody wanted to hear. It was the one thing that took the painful, awful connective tissue disorder that made Taryn's tissues and organs frail and fragile become something potentially terminal. Although the condition wasn't life threatening in and of itself, it came with a multitude of complications that caused chronic, often debilitating pain, and plagued her with symptoms that attacked each and every one of her systems.

There was no cure for EDS, but the various symptoms could be addressed and treated individually, even if the "treatment" was just a temporary fix.

When you threw in the complication of an aneurysm, however, the game changed. She'd hoped to avoid one, but there it was. And it was growing.

"Are you having any new symptoms?" her doctor asked.

Taryn shrugged. "I can feel the pulsating in my stomach more often. It hurts to eat too, but it always has so I wouldn't say that's *new*, necessarily."

"You're down ten pounds from last month."

"That might also be from the vomiting. I've been doing that a lot more."

"I can give you something to help that. Anything triggering the vomiting?"

"Nah," Taryn replied. "It's usually a little worse at night and right after big meals. I've been trying to eat smaller ones throughout the day."

"What about the tummy pain?"

"Mostly with eating. It's taken me out of the game a few times and I've had to lie down and keep still for a few hours, but nothing specific seems to trigger it. It just happens."

"You know that if you get that ripping, tearing feeling that doesn't feel like your 'normal' pain you need to go straight to the hospital," Dr. Culver warned her. "It probably won't be anything serious, but we don't want to risk it. We're at that stage now where we have to start worrying about ruptures and dissections."

"Is there *anything* we can do?"

"I've sent a referral to the cardiologist and gastroenterologist so you should be hearing from them soon.

Your last echo was abnormal and showed some mitral stenosis and general hypokinesis. We need to keep an eye on those things. We'll continue to monitor your blood pressure and try to keep your stress levels down, too. We *might* need to start talking surgery soon. It's risky for you with the EDS and it doesn't always work but it's something we don't want to rule out just yet. How's your pain level?"

So Taryn spent the next fifteen minutes talking about her options, describing her latest symptoms, and scheduling more tests.

Over the past year and a half. Her health had taken a dramatic turn, and she was still having trouble dealing with the new developments. As though seeing the past through her camera and communicating with the dead wasn't a big enough disruption, she now had these confounding medical issues to worry about.

And, as much as she wanted to ignore them, she couldn't. They were progressing and she was getting worse, like it or not.

With each passing month, the pain grew more difficult to manage, even with strong pain medication. It was becoming harder to walk, eating was no longer as fun as it had once been, and her energy levels were at an all-time low. She dutifully consumed her vitamins and supplements, was religious about taking her medications on time, ate a healthy diet (something that pained her since she did love her junk food), went through the physical therapy they sent her to, and did everything her EDS specialist recommended. She was a model patient.

And yet she continued to worsen.

Since there was no cure for Ehlers-Danlos Syndrome, however, she was basically putting a Band-Aid on everything until...

"Until I die," she muttered aloud as she trudged to her car, angry and frustrated. "I'm going to die and I *still* don't understand the ending of 'Lost.'"

Sometimes life just wasn't fair.

AKER, *TARYN* discovered, was more accommodating than she'd initially given him credit. After working with him for a little over a week she'd almost stopped apologizing every time she changed her schedule. Almost.

"Hey, sorry I didn't call," she spoke into her phone as she drove along Broadway through downtown. "I got held up at the doctor. Is it okay if we go now and work a few hours?"

"That's fine," he replied, his voice clipped but courteous.

"I'm on my way there but if you need some time I can–"

"I'll be there in fifteen minutes. I'm ready. Don't get out of your vehicle until I get there."

That was another thing, too. He was *always* ready. Taryn wondered if the man just sat by his phone, waiting for her to tell him she needed to go to the motel.

The thought was kinkier sounding than she'd intended.

The Nashville skyline rose above her as she flew across the bridge towards East Nashville. She could remember a time when she'd been afraid to venture to that part of town, a fear that was probably as much urban legend as anything. Now more and more houses were being renovated and the area was teeming with young professionals, families with children, and funky businesses.

Things changed. Taryn wasn't sure she always liked those changes but she was always happy to have new places to eat.

Over the course of the past week, she hadn't gotten much work done. She'd shown up twice to take pictures but the brutal rain had restricted her to the motel's interior. The interior, as luck would have it, was too dark without any natural light (the electricity was sporadic and mostly didn't work). The motel's open parking lot and motor lodge style didn't offer plentiful protection from the weather.

Plus, with the rain being so bad, there wasn't anywhere for Aker to go and still keep an eye on her. One afternoon he'd followed her into the small, cramped lobby to get out of the rain and that had been an uncomfortable experience for both parties involved.

Taryn was itching to get some real work done. She'd only taken a handful of pictures and none of them had been of the rooms. At the rate she was going, she was never going to get finished, much less meet her deadline.

The last thing she needed was a pissed off country singer. She'd never be allowed in the Ryman or Tootsie's again.

"I should have been sketching by now," she complained.

When her car rudely ignored her and didn't offer a response, she popped in a CD and turned Shooter Jennings up loud. She was in the mood to jam, despite the dismal news from her doctor.

Determined to make the most out of what was left of the day, Taryn sped down the road with her windows down, her hair flying back from her face. She couldn't do anything about the state of her health, but she *could* do her job. That was something, at least.

Aker, true to his word, showed up exactly fifteen minutes later. Taryn had barely pulled into the decrepit parking lot herself when his vehicle came sidling up next to hers.

"Better weather today, huh?" she asked with a smile.

"Huh," he grunted, which could have been interpreted any number of ways.

"I'm probably going to stay about two hours, is that okay?" she asked brightly, trying not to lose the smile she'd plastered on.

Taryn was determined to make this man like her. It had become a personal challenge.

"Take however long you need," he barked. He was already unfolding his chair and dragging out his cooler.

As Taryn started towards the motel's entrance, however, he jogged ahead of her. "Wait just a minute," Aker ordered as he passed her by, a set of keys jingling in his beefy hand.

Obligingly, Taryn stood back while he unlocked the door. She waited impatiently as he marched through the small rooms, checking the dark corners and peering into nooks and crannies.

"Like a little kid at bedtime, asking Daddy to look under the bed," she snorted.

Although, of course, Taryn's father had never been *that* kind of daddy. Aloof and lost in his own head much of the time, he'd had more time for academia than a young daughter who might be afraid of the boogeyman.

She'd checked her *own* closets.

When Aker gave her the "all clear" sign, Taryn flashed him a thumbs up and entered the lobby.

She'd upgraded to an iPod fairly recently and was enjoying slowly adding her vast music collection to it. Heart was currently blasting from the tiny speakers but to set the mood she turned on Parker Brown. The song was about pine trees and being close to nature—or so she thought, he was a little elusive. For all she knew it could've been about his pet parrot. Ruby Jane sang backup and their voices blended in perfect harmony, soaring over the instruments and twisting and turning around one another until you couldn't tell where one started and the other began.

Taryn had downloaded his albums the night before and uploaded Ruby's from the CDs she already owned. She wanted to listen to them sing while she worked. It seemed right.

In spite of the sunlight, which probably only *felt* brighter since it had been so dreary lately, the room was still gloomy. Taryn couldn't imagine the place feeling welcoming to anyone, even back before it was essentially a flop house.

"There must have been a time when it was okay," she said aloud. "I need to check out some old pictures of it."

Her voice got lost in the stuffiness and tepid darkness, but it was still reassuring to hear it.

"I might go crazy, but at least I have myself to keep me company," she giggled.

The song changed to "Close Up the Honky Tonks," a Buck Owens cover. The upbeat melody gave Taryn a boost of energy and she found herself working faster with the increased drive.

As she walked around and took her shots, she tried to imagine Parker Brown staying in such a place, and even weirder, *Ruby Jane* being there with him. Although, of course, Ruby had her house in Nashville; she had no real reason to spend the night at the Black Raven–unless the rumors about her and Parker had been true.

"Everyone thinks they had a thing going up until he died," she'd informed Matt. "At this point it's just assumed."

"Why?" he'd asked, reasonably enough, so it had Taryn pausing.

"Well, I guess because they had such great chemistry. The pictures of them together, their singing, and all the song lyrics she wrote about him after he died."

"How do you know they're about him?"

Sometimes his logic frustrated her. Why did he have to be so darn reasonable?

"Because," she'd stammered. "They're about loving someone and them being gone. Like, gone as in *death*."

"Hmmm..."

She knew what he wanted to say, that since she'd lost someone herself she read death into everything. And, the fact was, he might have been right.

But I'm also right about this, she thought. Parker had died before she was born but even a fool could see and hear the love between the two.

No way was that superficial Matt, she thought smugly.

"I clearly need a life," she mumbled. "I'm walking around mentally examining the love life between a dead person and my boss."

Even worse, she was having a make-believe argument with Matt.

Taryn let herself get back to the task at hand. She couldn't see the elegant Ruby being comfortable on one of the rickety chairs or what she imagined were hard, unforgiving mattresses. Even as a young woman in her twenties, Ruby had been sophisticated and looked every inch the lady, especially next to her fellow band mates who looked like they'd just robbed a motorcycle gang. It was as much Ruby's elegance and beauty against their rough edges and wild reputation as it was their innovative style of country music that had given Silver Streak its fame.

Given its location on a main road, the motel was unnaturally quiet. Taryn felt like she could've been on an isolated mountaintop rather than downtown Nashville. As she got lost in her work she became even more focused on surroundings, the idea of Aker's presence waiting outside and the faint sounds of passing vehicles drifted away. Miss Dixie provided a special rhythm for her that fell instantly in tune with and as Taryn moved from room to room, trying different angles and taking shots, she fell into her own little world, lulled by the "clicks" and flashes of light.

It was the closest she ever got to meditating, and the most relaxed she ever felt.

When she entered the small break room with the fetid mattress and garbage-covered table, Taryn turned in slow circles to ensure she captured the entire space. A rustling sound from one of the corners had her surprised and she hesitated, finger half pressed down on the button.

She couldn't make out much more than the outlines of the furniture in the darkness, but when the noise came again, this time louder, a shadow materialized on the wall in front of her. As the rustling sound increased, filling the room with a crackling that was as painful as fingernails on a chalkboard, the hefty shadow grew and grew until it was nearly as tall and wide as Taryn herself. She watched in fascinated horror as the darkness of the silhouette swirled and seemed to move inside its boundaries. Then, in a movement that should have been impossible, it seemed to *leap* at her, coming clear off the wall.

"Eeeekkk!" Taryn screamed, her voice muffled by the room's stillness and dampness. In a reflex move, her finger pushed down on her camera, filling the space with the bright light of Miss Dixie's flash.

Wasting no time for answers, Taryn turned to run and collided straight into the wall behind her, tripping over the large sewer rat that was also trying to escape the airless space.

"Miss Magill!" Aker's voice boomed from the lobby. "Everything okay?"

Embarrassed, Taryn clutched her head in both hands and leaned against the wall. "In here. I'm okay."

When Aker found her, she was rubbing at her temples and cursing. "What happened?"

"I heard a noise and saw a shadow," she explained. "I thought it was—well, I don't know what I *thought* it was. It just turned out to be a rat, though. An enormous rat, like a 1970's horror movie kind of rat that's been eating radioactive cheese, but still just a rat. He's gone now."

"Would you like for me to find the vandal?" Aker demanded, face lined in determination.

"'*Vandal*?'" Taryn croaked. "It's a rat. I think it will be okay. I'll be ready for the sucker next time."

Although Aker did not look convinced, he left her alone and went back to man his post.

"A damn rat," she shook her head, embarrassed with herself. She'd done some foolish things on jobs before, but she didn't usually have a witness. That was going to take some getting used to.

FIGURING *SHE'D* done about all of the administrative parts of the motel there were to do, Taryn wrapped things up and went back outside. The sun was starting to drop down over the buildings in the distance; soon the moon would make an appearance and then she'd lose all her natural light. She needed to get her butt in gear.

"A walk around the perimeter. I can finish that up today, too," she told herself.

To Aker, she hollered, "Hey dude! I'm gonna walk around the motel and take some shots. I won't go in anywhere!"

He hesitated as though he might get up and accompany her, but then he apparently decided she was safe enough, what with the wall and gate surrounding the property, and settled back into his chair. Taryn noticed, however, that he didn't pick up his book or magazine. He might not be following her, but he was remaining alert.

"Who the heck *is* he?" she wondered, not for the first time. Besides a hire-a-former-cop bodyguard?

Taryn had made her way all the way around to the back of the motel when she remembered her camera and the picture she'd inadvertently taken of the wall when the rat dashed out.

She stopped walking and turned on Miss Dixie. It was the last shot on her card.

The small break room was no longer dark. Instead, it was full of artificial light, supplied by the overhead light and small lamp that rested on a side table.

The bed still looked ratty and it wasn't anything she would sleep on, but it was cleanish. A wool blanket was pulled up over the stained mattress. The table was clear of clutter, save a plate of what looked like pasta and a cup of something. A worn area rug covered most of the floor.

There was no sign of the rat or the shadow.

"Well, that's interesting anyway," Taryn said with a little laugh.

She might have been making light of what she was viewing, but the truth was that she was incredibly unnerved. She never got used to seeing the past in this way, of seeing the things Miss Dixie revealed. It was a shock to her system each time.

And a big part of Taryn was afraid that one day *she'd* get sucked into the picture herself, with nobody to drag her back out.

"What do you want me to do with this?" She spoke to the motel but it remained aloof and stoic. If it had an agenda, it wasn't revealing it.

Taryn wrapped her arms around her chest and swallowed hard. She couldn't imagine a scenario in which anything good came out of her working with the motel's inner demons.

"Maybe it's just a fluke," she whispered to Miss Dixie. "Maybe I am just picking up random things and it doesn't mean anything."

For the time being, she would make herself believe that.

The back of the motel was in far worse shape than the front. From the back, she could see how the building had deteriorated over the years and really gone downhill. Management had obviously done nothing to keep up pretenses back there since nobody could see it from the road or parking lot.

The building was a square, with five rooms on each side for a grand total of twenty. The five that faced the back were the worst of the lot. The ones in front had at least been renovated in the past twenty years.

The back rooms, which seemed to house long-term residents when the motel was functioning, could only be entered from the courtyard, while visitors could drive up to their doors on the other fifteen. The motel had never had central heat and air installed and had relied on individual A/C units in the summertime. None of them remained; Taryn had heard that vandals had stolen them for the copper and metal, which evidently fetched a good price if you didn't mind taking the unit apart.

Still, although they were missing they'd left their marks behind. Literally. Over the years, runoff from the machines had dripped down from the windows, leaving a discolored stain in their trail. Plywood was still nailed onto the walls and windows, a sign that the units hadn't fit properly and the owner had simply patched up the empty space with whatever wood was handy. In some cases, the windows were missing or had been broken; ratty curtains billowed out from the empty rooms like emaciated arms beckoning passersby.

It was clear that the back had not been painted for many years. The wood back there was a crazy shade of yellow, almost orange in some places. Vines grew up the side of the building and, in some cases, *through* the building. Nature was slowly starting to take over as if to say, "Leave something unattended long enough and we'll take it back!"

The grass was tall, wild, the weeds nearly up to Taryn's waist. She took pictures of the roof and its many holes and unmatched patches, broken windows, vines, billowing curtains, and broken drainpipes. She stopped below a gutter that had an actual tree growing from it and stood, mesmerized, at just how quickly things could go downhill if someone weren't there to take care of them.

At last, she worked all the way around the square, taking pictures of the doors and exterior. By the time she finished, it was twilight and Aker was starting to look pointedly at his watch. She still hadn't been inside a room, or inside the courtyard.

"Weather's meant to be good tomorrow. Want to get an early start?" she asked as they both began packing up.

"That's fine. So do you want to meet here at 7? 8?" he asked.

Taryn snorted. "Okay, when I said 'early' I really just meant before noon. How about 10?"

Aker nodded. "That's fine. I'll see you here at 10."

Although they packed up at the same time and got in their cars in unison, Taryn noted that he waited until she pulled out onto the main road before he left.

"OH *SWEETIE*, I'm so sorry," Matt said softly.

Taryn, stretched out in a hot bubble bath, groaned. When Matt resorted to the traditional pet names, rather than the goofy ones he'd cooked up himself, like 'my queen' or something *Star Trek* oriented, she knew things were bad.

"We just know that it has grown," she said, letting the hot water relax her muscles and take away some of the aches and pains. "The doctor didn't say I was going to die tomorrow or anything."

"Is there anything I can do?" he asked quietly.

Taryn could imagine Matt sitting in his living room, long legs outstretched before him, a Sci-Fi movie on low in the background. Knowing him, he'd probably cooked up something gourmet or had stopped and picked up Cajun on his way home from work—a far cry from the microwaveable macaroni and cheese that she'd had for dinner. She suddenly wanted to be there with him, snuggling in next to him and watching whatever apocalyptic movie he had on for entertainment.

As if he could read her mind, Matt asked, "Do you want me to come up there?"

Taryn hesitated and almost told him "yes" but then stopped.

"No, that's okay," she frowned at her stubborn pride. "I'll see you in a few weeks. I've got this job to do and am already behind and you've got your students. I'll be okay."

"You want to talk about it?"

The fact that Matt, who could sometimes get lost in his head and not always empathize, was worried about her almost scared her more than what the doctor had told her. Matt had always had a sixth sense where she was concerned, even when they were kids. It made Taryn nervous.

"Not really," she replied. "Not yet. I'm still processing, I think."

"You want to tell me about the new job then?"

"Okay, do you know something I don't? Like I'm going to kick the bucket tomorrow or something? Because you almost never ask me about the project," she laughed.

"I just thought it might take your mind off it."

So Taryn began telling him about the motel, going into the grisly details of the structure's appearance and care. "To be honest, it's kind of a mundane job," she finished. "I mean, there's nothing really interesting about the building, other than its history and my employer. The building itself is just your average roadside motel. Well, your average abandoned roadside motel. There are probably a thousand like them in the desert out west."

"So you think it will be an easy job?" he asked tentatively. "No, well, you know..."

Taryn bit her lip. "I don't know. I haven't looked at my pictures yet."

She wasn't ready to tell him about the one in the break room. No reason to worry him any more than she already had.

"Why not?"

"Because maybe I'm afraid of what I'll find?" It was a question more than a statement.

"You think there's something there?" he pressed. Matt knew all about the things that had happened on her other jobs. Indeed, he had been there for some of the occurrences.

"I don't know yet," she admitted. "I haven't seen or felt anything but I know the stories. And once I...oh, it sounds silly."

"No," Matt urged her to continue. "It's not silly. Once you what?"

"If there is something there then once I look at the pictures and see it then I'll be a part of it," she finished lamely. "And then I can't turn back."

"The jobs that need the most work seem to find you and pick you," Matt said carefully. "Is that what you're thinking? That perhaps this job called to you and if you delve into too far you'll be caught up in something else again?"

"Yes!" Taryn all but shouted in agreement. Sometimes it felt really good to have someone in her life who totally "got" her.

"I know how that must make you feel," he said. "I know how it makes me feel. I worry about you. I worry with each thing that happens that it's going to be too much for you, that you're going to buckle eventually. Not that you're not strong but, well, there's only so much a single person can stand."

"Things have been so *good* lately," Taryn said. "I've been so happy and peaceful. I don't know that I am ready to rock that boat."

As if in agreement, her bubbles began popping in clumps, leaving her in a murky film. Her water had lost its warmth.

SIX

Taryn *stood before Room #5* and observed it with interest.

There might have been twenty rooms at the Black Raven Inn, but only one of them was famous. Only one of them had seen the death of a celebrity.

She'd only been commissioned to paint this one.

The room didn't look any different than the others from the outside. All the doors looked identical, with varying degrees of neglect, wear, and tear. There was nothing exceptional about Room #5 from where she stood.

Still, her fingers trembled slightly as she clutched Miss Dixie to her chest. If there was something inside the motel, it was in this room. This was the one the investigators were interested in, the one the paranormal fans had stumbled over themselves to stay in.

"I can't turn back once I go inside," she whispered to herself, lest Aker heard her and thought she was nutty.

Taryn was no stranger to the supernatural. She'd seen more than her fair share of haunted places, had been targeted by ghosts and other unexplainable forces. Yet, in most of those cases, she'd walked into the situation with blind eyes. The Black Raven Inn was different; it was known for being famous.

Despite the establishment's rough reputation, the room never had any trouble finding visitors when it was open. Its famous occupant had garnered a cult following and many of those fans, some fellow musicians, had flocked to stay in the place where he'd taken his last breath. They'd even built a little shrine to him in the courtyard; Taryn was going to take a look at that next.

The paranormal investigators had come as well. They'd brought their video camera and EVP equipment and whatever else they used and attempted to make contact with the young man who hadn't been able to resist the urges of the dark mistress who dealt him her fatal kiss.

Taryn knew all about those people, the ones who had ignored the drug deals and prostitutes and occasional domestic disputes so that they could stay in their fallen idol's room.

"It would be like me staying in Graceland," she said aloud, trying to put herself in a position of understanding.

And now, here she was, standing inches from the door itself. If the rumors were true, if the room were haunted, then she'd be exposing herself to something she might not be able to walk away from.

"Well," she sighed with resignation. "Maybe he's a friendly ghost anyway."

The key clicked in the lock and she let herself in.

PARKER *BROWN'S* room was much smaller than she'd anticipated.

The king-sized bed took up most of the floor space so Taryn found herself all but turning sideways to walk to the other side of the room. There wasn't much light filtering through the dusty window but she found that the electric was having a good day and decided to come one.

The broken light fixture above provided little in the way of illumination but it did cast away a few of the darker shadows.

A small television stand held a model from the 1980s. Rabbit ears extended from a dinosaur screen with a hairline crack down the middle. Someone had left a bottle of maroon-colored nail polish on top of the grimy surface.

Two nightstands flanked the bed with the saggy mattress and stained, floral quilt that was partway pulled back, like someone was getting ready for bed. A rodent had left a copious amount of droppings on the quilt. At some point it looked like something had started to make a nest on one of the nightstands and then given up, as if the room was too depressing to make any kind of permanent home in.

Although the room didn't have a closet, it did have a small alcove with a curtain rod in which wire hangers dangled. A beat-up bureau rested under the rod, two of its drawers gaping open.

Taryn walked over to one of the closed doors and opened it nervously. Even though Aker had thoroughly checked the room before she arrived that morning, she'd seen enough horror movies to worry about such things.

Inside was a microscopic bathroom with a sink that could be reached from the toilet and a shower with a mildew-splattered plastic curtain. The toilet and sink looked original to the room. For a moment Taryn stood there and let the realization of where she was sink in.

"Huh," she said, taking in the confined space.

It was a morbid thought but Parker Brown had, at one time, stood in that very spot. He'd washed his hands and brushed his teeth in that sink. He had used the now filthy toilet. She was looking at a room that had not changed in forty years, seeing it the same way he would have. That was about as close to time travel as most people would ever get.

Taryn shivered at the thought.

"A goose walked over your grave," she could all but hear her grandmother, Stella, telling her.

A goose or a *ghost*?

Back in the bedroom Taryn leaned against the cold wall and studied the space again. The floor was tile, stained and scuffed from years of use and abuse. An old wall heater was the only heat source. The window unit in the back was still intact in this room. Its bulky frame filled most of the window, blocking out the light on that side. There was another closed door that led to the courtyard. She'd go out there in a minute.

A threadbare area rug covered most of the floor. It was impossible to see the original pattern or color.

For the most part, the room was a cold, sad, lonely sight...if not for the walls.

She hadn't expected the room to hold onto the mementos that visitors had left behind. She guessed she thought they would've been carted away or even trashed when the motel closed.

Room #5 was a veritable memorial to Parker Brown.

A large poster of him and the band, advertising a show in Tulsa, hung over the bed. Faded pictures printed off the computer covered the wall above the television stand. Two of his album covers were nailed above the nightstands. Here and there, scattered without thought to design, were pieces of paper with handwritten song lyrics to some of his most popular tunes. Framed photographs adorned the room and, stuck between the plastic and glass, were dozens of guitar picks people had left behind. A framed picture of him set on the nightstand, turned to face the very spot he'd died in.

"That's a little creepy," Taryn said. Something about the picture's position didn't set right with her so she walked over to it, picked it up, and turned it to face the other direction. Now Parker was looking towards the door, not his death bed.

Most captivating were the personal messages that had been written on the walls and furniture. They'd been left behind in ink, marker, pencil, and even fingernail polish and what appeared to be lipstick. Personal memories of Parker, original poems and song lyrics penned by artists who'd stayed in the room, thank you notes for songs that had gotten the writer through a tough time, experiences visitors had had in the room...

Taryn turned and looked at the wall behind her where she'd been leaning. There were half a dozen messages scrawled there. She leaned forward and read one written in what appeared to be a red Sharpie:

"Stayed here 09/05/98. Woke up in the middle of the night and saw a ball of light in the corner of the room. Watched it bounce around the room and then hover over the television.

Swore I heard someone strumming the guitar. I'll never forget the feeling that someone else was in the room with me."

Taryn winced and wrapped her arms around her chest, a defense mechanism she'd used since she was a child. She wished she'd left the door open. In the tiny, cramped space she was starting to feel claustrophobic.

Another message read:

"As I was drifting off to sleep I heard a voice close to my ear whispering 'Hello.' I slept with the TV and lamp on but when I woke up in the night to go to the bathroom both had been turned off."

And then, simply:

"Parker Brown's music saved my life."

They'd come to that dreadful room to feel connected to him, to get as close to their idol as they could ever be. They'd all been trying to capture some of his essence, his energy.

"Did you know how much you were loved?" she asked the room.

Or was it that he was only loved because he was dead?

Damn, I'm getting cynical. Taryn shook her head.

It was time to get to work, though.

Taryn spent the next fifteen minutes capturing every inch of the room, in her own way trying to capture its essence in much the same way that the overnight visitors had. She took wide shots of the room and furnishings and then zoomed in on many of the messages, focusing on the uplifting ones as much as she could since she knew Ruby Jane would be viewing the photos.

By the time she finished, she was coughing and sneezing from a combination of the cold air and stuffiness, combined with the mold and dust and rodent excrement. Aside from the environmental factors of the motel's age and neglect, however, she wasn't feeling anything unusual.

Taryn breathed a sigh of relief. Perhaps the ghost stories were just that—*stories*. Tales made up by people who wanted to feel and see something that proved their hero wasn't completely gone.

When she was finished she went out the back door and entered the courtyard.

AS *EXPECTED*, the small shrine to Parker stood erect a few feet from the patio. Two rotting benches that once boasted blood-red paint bordered the wooden cross bearing his name. Beer and wine bottles had been left behind, as well as statues of crosses, the Virgin Mary, angels in various poses, and folded hands in prayers. Hundreds of guitar picks were scattered about, some faded by the sun and rain. Everything had a slight film over it, damaged from being left unattended to the elements.

She thought there was something poignant about the little shrine, about the people who were heartbroken enough to find their way to the motel and leave such things behind.

Taryn took pictures of the small memorial and then walked around, getting shots of other doors that opened to the enclosed space.

With a good budget and landscaper the courtyard might have been charming. A few trees grew in the middle and picnic tables with charcoal grills rotted beside them. Under the right circumstances she could easily see flowering plants, leafy shades, and musicians sharing songs and drinking together in the moonlight.

Now, however, it was a cheerless abandoned wasteland, littered with used needles, empty fast food cartons, and broken tree limbs.

Beautiful, abandoned and derelict houses broke Taryn's heart. The ones that were neglected tugged at her in the same way some people fell apart at the sight of abused animals.

Black Raven Inn bothered her in a different way. Here, she saw what *could* have been but never was. The potential of the place was reflected in the kind of crowd that had gathered there—desperate and, in many cases, hopeless.

"What brought you here, Parker? What were you doing here?" At the sound of her voice, a nearby Styrofoam cup was lifted gently into the air and floated past her face on a breeze. She watched it drift across the courtyard where it was deposited against a window. It landed with a soft sound.

Parker had family money, even without the band's success. He could have done better. What had brought him to the Black Raven Inn? What had kept bringing him back?

Taryn left the courtyard with a great weight resting on her shoulders. Such a place didn't deserve someone like Ruby Jane. There was too much sadness there, too much heaviness. Nobody needed that.

Taryn was usually against the destruction of history but in this case she thought tearing the motel down would be in everyone's best interest.

Feeling unsettled and a little dejected, she let herself back into Room #5 and locked the courtyard door behind her. As she crossed the room to leave, however, a cold dagger stabbed her through the chest, leaving her winded and shocked.

"Oof!" she gasped, grasping at her chest and shaking her head from the blast of pain.

Doubled over from the throbbing, Taryn paused and attempted to collect herself while the waves of bitter air gathered around her, chilling her to the bone. This was different from the coldness that she'd felt earlier. This time it was wet and probing, trying to penetrate her clothing and skin and sink inside of her. The acrid smell of filth increased and churned around her, making her gag and cough until acid rose in her throat and nose.

Taryn looked up, trying to find a reason for what was happening. Her eyes landed on Parker's picture on the nightstand. It was turned back around, facing the bed again.

The cold slowly began lifting from her, the pain easing up as the room returned to normal. When the feeling subsided and she could move again Taryn sprinted for the exit, fumbling for the key.

The heavy hand that gripped her shoulder from behind as she flung open the door was pure ice.

"Hello," it rasped in a voice neither male nor female.

The breath that rained down on her neck reeked of the grave.

SEVEN

Taryn was busy uploading her photos to be edited when the ringing of her phone startled her. The only person who ever called her was Matt, she conducted business through email, but it wasn't his ring tone.

"If you're wanting money from me you're going to have to wait in line," she called as she stalked across the floor to where the phone was charging in the wall.

When she saw the caller ID, however, her face lit up.

"David!" Her voice was filled with genuine warmth as she answered.

"There's my favorite ghost chaser," came the smooth, deep reply.

Taryn had met David earlier that year while working at an upscale resort on Jekyll Island off the coast of Georgia. He'd been working there as an anthropologist and they'd bonded over ghosts, alligators, and other assorted adventures.

He'd also saved her life, but not before Matt had been certain he had designs on her and Taryn was almost equally certain he was trying to kill her. One of them had been wrong.

"I thought you'd forgotten about me," she chided him as she settled onto the floor, her phone still plugged into the outlet.

"Never," he laughed. "I've just been up to my nose in work. I do have some news, though."

"What's up?"

"I'm going to be in *your* neck of the woods in two weeks. I'm doing a lecture at Belmont Mansion, part of the university's convocation series, and will be talking about our finds on the island. I was hoping we might be able to get together and have dinner while I'm in town," he said.

Taryn could feel the tinges of excitement edging around her. "Are you kidding? I don't just want to have dinner, I want to come to your lecture!"

"I don't know. It might be boring. I'm a scientist, not much of a speaker," he warned her.

"Oh please," Taryn scoffed.

It didn't matter what he said; once those college girls got a look at his dark skin, long ebony hair, and beautiful smile they'd be putty in his hands. David, full-blooded Creek Indian, was one of the most beautiful men she'd ever seen off the movie screen.

"I don't know much about Nashville so I'll leave it to you to find us a place to eat and hang out," he told her.

"Sure. Where are you staying?"

"Someplace downtown. Has a color in the name of it," he said.

"Hotel Indigo probably. It's one of those new, hip places."

"I probably won't fit in very well then," David laughed. "I haven't been hip in at least ten years."

"You'll be fine, I promise. I'll find something within walking distance of it."

They spent the next few minutes chatting about his work and the discoveries on Jekyll Island. Taryn had spent several months living between it and St. Simon's and they had been some of the best months of her life. Having David nearby, someone she could grab for the occasional dinner and day trip, had been icing on the cake to a summer that was relaxing and productive. Although she hadn't worked once her job finished on Jekyll, when she moved over to the house on St. Simon's she had used her time to paint, take photographs, and read at leisure without a thought to bills or money.

As someone who had held a full-time job since she was sixteen and sometimes worked all day and throughout the night, she'd never had a time like that in her life, a time all to herself. It was wonderful.

"So what are you up to right now?" David asked at last.

Taryn leaned back against the wall, relaxed and happy to have someone to chat with after a long day. "Well, guess who my current employer is?"

He let out a long, slow whistle when she told him Ruby's name. "Look at you! How'd you swing that?"

"She was familiar with my work," Taryn explained. "She found me through a project I worked on with Andrew a long time ago."

"Wow, that's awesome. I am so impressed. My granny was a huge fan. I can remember Ruby Jane being on the Ralph Emery Show when I was a kid. I loved her, I reckon it was that kind of high-pitched squeaky voice of hers, and Granny always let me stay up late when she was a guest." David laughed. "It was such a big deal back then. I can still remember Granny in her rocker, shucking corn or stringing beans, and me pulling all the cushions off the couch to make a pillow fort. Ruby's kind of the soundtrack to my childhood."

"Mine too," Taryn agreed. She was thrilled to have someone to talk about her love of music, and of Ruby, with. "You know, that duet's album she did just about changed my life. I can remember right after my parents died I was in a real low place and nothing could get me out of that funk. It went on for months. Then one night I put on that CD and fell asleep listening to it. First time I'd slept through the night since their death."

"I love the way country music fans form such special relationships with the artists they like. Sometimes I feel like I know the people. I guess that would be creepy to them," David mused.

Taryn laughed. "Probably, but I do the same thing. Oh! And guess where I'm working? Black Raven Inn."

David was silent for a moment and then, when he replied, his voice was quiet. "You mean the place where..."

"Yep."

"Damn," he whistled again. "I figured they'd tear that place down. Actually, I guess I thought they *had*."

"Yeah, well, they *should*. It's kind of a hellhole," Taryn agreed. "But it's also interesting in its own ugly, creepy kind of way."

"So how's *that* going?"

"I haven't really gotten into the meat of the work yet. I'm still taking pictures. It's been an experience, though. Oh, and I have a bodyguard!"

"Considering some of the things that have happened to you on the job, I think that's probably a good idea." David laughed. "So, don't leave me hanging. It's like you're working for Dolly Parton or Reba McEntire or something. This is *huge*! I want to bask in your glory and live vicariously through you. What's she like? Is she pretty in person? Hateful? Funny? Weird? A good friend would spill the beans."

"I've only met her in person once but I *am* seeing her again in the morning. She's very," Taryn paused, searching for the right description, "I guess the word is elegant. Tall, willowy, looks like she might break if you breathed on her too hard. But she's also well-spoken and polite. One of those people that you just know is intelligent the moment they start talking. She seems to be into all of these books on different cultures and religions, very well read. Maybe a little reserved."

"I like her already. Doesn't seem like the kind of person who would've run around with a bunch of outlaws back in the day?" David laughed.

"Ha! Not at all. I keep trying to reconcile the idea of the Ruby I've met with the Ruby who was a member of the Silver Streak band, with Parker, but it's hard. Like two totally different people."

"I guess we were all different in our younger days. I was a fan of Parker's," David said. "I have all three of Silver Streak's albums and they got me through some tough times. A real shame that he died so young, along with so many others like Joplin and Morrison and Hank Sr. The drugs, man. Some just can't handle their fame."

Taryn nodded her head in agreement, even though he couldn't see her.

"Just be careful, okay?" David warned her. "Guard yourself. I've heard stories about that place. And even if it's not haunted, a lot of lonely souls with *real* problems fell apart within those walls. You don't know what they left behind and what's still living there."

"You think there's something wrong with the hotel?"

"I don't know," David replied thoughtfully. "Maybe. Sometimes bad places draw in good people and change them. Sometimes people with problems are naturally drawn to the same location, an exchange of energy so to speak. Either way, I don't want anything to happen to you."

Taryn shook as she remembered the clerk's words in the camera store. He'd said nearly the same thing.

Could a *place* really be bad without reason?

TARYN *BANGED* her head down on her desk and scrubbed at the back of her neck with her hand. A headache was forming from staring at the laptop screen for so long. A carry-out container of Greek food was growing cold by her keyboard and a reality TV program blasted obscenities a few feet away. (She liked the company.) She'd been staring at her pictures all afternoon, trying to edit them in a way that made them look presentable to her employer.

"The pressure is on," she moaned into her arms.

Taryn could feel Miss Dixie drolly watching her from across the room. She could almost hear her saying, *I did* my *job. Now it's your turn not to screw it up.*

Sometimes the pictures of her worksite had the place looking better than it did in reality. Through her eyes and Miss Dixie's lens she could capture the essence of the building while ignoring the neglect and poor condition.

That was not the case for the Black Raven Inn.

If anything, her pictures made it look *worse*. Taryn wouldn't have thought that was possible and now she cringed at the implication.

Am I going to be able to make it look good at all, she wondered.

Not without ample use of her imagination. "I'm gonna have to dig deep in my well of ingenuity to make this happen," she grumbled.

She'd taken more than three-hundred photographs in all, so far. The best ones were of the exterior, although she had a few good shots of the lobby. She hadn't started on the ones of Room #5 yet. She needed some Tylenol and a fresh dose of caffeine before she attacked those.

Two weeks into the job and she still wasn't real sure what she was doing or which direction she should go in. First the weather had held her up and then her health. A severe lack of motivation was starting to set in.

"I gotta start sketching tomorrow," she reminded herself as she got up and stretched. It wasn't doing her any good to sit there and stare at the screen anymore. She was starting to see things that weren't there.

Taryn rooted through her refrigerator, searching for a Coke she hoped was stuck somewhere behind the assorted food cartons. Once she started sketching, the job would move along quickly. She'd spend time with the charcoals and then, once satisfied, she'd bring out the oil paints. The Black Raven Inn demanded oils. Watercolors were too whimsical for such a place.

"A ha!" Upon finding the last Coke she'd hidden from herself, Taryn stood up with glee and held her treasure in the air. "Found you!"

She needed to make a run to the store. There was no way she could get through the night without more caffeine. She rarely drank, had never smoked, and was only mildly addicted to bad TV. Caffeine was her main vice; she couldn't live without it.

Back in the living room she turned the channel to something more subdued and then settled into her office chair again.

"Let's start Round Two!" She liked cheering herself on sometimes. When nobody else was around to do it for you, you had to dig the motivation out yourself.

The first few pictures of Room #5 were unremarkable. The room appeared small, dingy, and cramped. That's also the way it looked in real life. The fading and curling posters of Parker, which looked even sadder in her photographs than she remembered them looking in reality, were still on the walls and nightstands.

And then she came to one she'd taken by accident.

Taryn was about to hang it up for the night when a shot she didn't remember taking jumped onto the screen and had her leaning in for a closer look. Unbeknownst to her, Taryn's camera had been jostled to the right when Miss Dixie had gone off. It must have happened when she was trying to leave, when she'd been doubled over in pain.

Pointing towards the bathroom door, the photo was at an awkward angle—cutting off most of the floor and getting a good piece of the popcorn ceiling. What it *did* manage to capture in the shot, however, had Taryn shaking.

The unmistakable figure of a man stood by the door, leaning against the flimsy wood in a similar way Taryn had later leaned against the wall herself, just inches from where he stood. Most of his facial features were unclear. However, she could still make out the loose-fitting pants, shaggy hair, and long delicate fingers on hands that fell to his sides. His shoulders were slumped as though he carried the weight of the world. From the neck up, however, he was confident. His head was raised and held high and although she couldn't make out his nose or mouth, it was clear that his piercing eyes were staring straight into her camera.

Although she had felt nothing of his presence at that time, he'd been all too aware of Taryn's.

EIGHT

Taryn stood on Ruby Jane's porch and shifted nervously from one hip to the other, trying desperately to ignore the sharp pain that shot down her leg. In her hands she carried her laptop, as well as a spare memory card with most of the images from the motel.

Most of them...

She still wasn't sure how much she should show Ruby, or how much she should *tell* her.

"I wouldn't show her the picture from the room," Matt had advised her the night before.

Taryn had called him around midnight, at odds with herself on how to proceed with the picture. Should she tell Ruby? Show her? Keep it to herself for awhile to see if it happened again? She didn't know how to proceed.

"Are you *sure*? Do you not think that's something she would want to see?" Taryn worried.

"Just think about it," Matt replied. "What if she's not a believer in these things? What if she thinks you're trying to pull a prank on her? Or even extort her in some way?"

Taryn scowled, feeling discouraged. Matt was the main voice of reason in her life and sometimes it was annoying, especially when he was right.

"But what if she *is* a believer?" Taryn countered at last.

"Then something like this might hurt her," Matt said carefully. "How would *you* feel if someone took a picture and captured Andrew? Or Stella?"

Hurt, Taryn answered silently. *I'd feel hurt.*

For one thing, she'd never be able to understand why someone other than herself had been able to make contact with her fiancé and grandmother when *she* couldn't. (And not from lack of trying, either. It was a hurtful fact that Taryn had been able to make contact with a number people who had passed on, and yet none of them were departed souls who were personal to Taryn.)

After spending several stressful hours studying the photo and chewing on Matt's words she ultimately decided not to share the image. Matt was right; Ruby Jane didn't know her and she was concerned Ruby might think Taryn was trying to extort her or just be funny, and Taryn didn't want that.

Now she found herself outside, waiting to be let in.

"Taryn." Ruby smiled as she opened the door. "I've been anxiously awaiting your visit all morning!"

Today Ruby was dressed in a flowing peasant skirt with a lightweight sweater that hung loosely on her lithe frame. Her long gray hair was wound up in a loose bun but her flawless complexion with nary a wrinkle and the horn-rimmed glasses made her look decades younger. From a distance, Taryn thought she could have passed for a teenager.

"Pardon the mess," Ruby called as she led Taryn into the living room. "I've got a benefit with the Humane Society coming up tomorrow and I'm trying to fold brochures and stuff envelopes."

Sure enough, the coffee table and surrounding chairs were covered with leaflets. "Just clear yourself off a spot," Ruby said as she began making room for Taryn's laptop.

Taryn grinned, pleased by the fact that the celebrity could be as messy as anyone else she knew.

"Now I've got around two-hundred photographs for you to take a look at," Taryn warned her as she waited for the computer to boot. "I also brought you your SD card with the images on them as well, so you can keep copies for yourself."

Ruby held out her hand to accept the card. When their fingers touched, though, Taryn felt a buzzing sensation and recoiled in surprise.

"I'm sorry," Ruby apologized. "I seem to be picking up a lot of static."

Taryn studied her curiously, remembering the similar shock she'd received at the motel. It was fall, however, and static *was* in the air.

Still...

For a millisecond when Taryn had looked at Ruby she'd seen not the woman before her in the skirt and bun, but a younger version of her with long wavy hair and a toothy grin.

"The computer's ready if you'd like to take a look," Taryn offered, unable to take her eyes off Ruby.

Something's happening, she thought. *I'm not sure what it is, but it's fascinating.*

If Ruby saw or felt anything peculiar then she kept it to herself.

A door down the hall opened and the creak was a foreign sound, as though another dimension was opening.

Moments later Taryn heard footsteps padding towards them. When she looked up, Lenny Parsons was standing before them.

"Lenny," Ruby said absently, "this is Taryn. She's the artist I was telling you about."

The man who stood before them was one of the best-selling solo artists of all time. Although he'd once been a part of Silver Streak with Ruby and Parker, after Parker's death he'd gone out on his own. He was outsold only by Michael Jackson, Garth Brooks, and Elvis. He'd even outsold Madonna.

And now he was standing within mere inches of Taryn, wearing nothing but a bathrobe and house slippers.

"Nice to meet you," he replied casually. He was in his late sixties but still had a youthful looking body. He was also still gorgeously dangerous, with jet black hair, bright blue eyes, and tanned skin.

Taryn was back to feeling like she might faint.

"He's got a show at the Ryman tonight," Ruby said.

"A tribute show," Lenny added. "It will be a little embarrassing."

"Oh, you know you're going to eat it up. I'll be singing," she informed Taryn. "And telling everyone how much I love him."

"Lies, all lies," Lenny grinned.

When he excused himself from the room, Ruby made a face that was difficult to read. "He stays here with me when he comes to town. Says he likes it better than a hotel room. We've been friends for almost fifty years. And after what happened to Parker, well...I don't like my men to get very far from me. I'm a bit like a mother hen in that respect."

Taryn understood. Sometimes she felt like she was slowly weaning herself from Matt for the same reason—it hurt too much to worry about someone so much.

TARYN *SPENT* most of the afternoon scrolling through the numerous photos with Ruby, pointing out the ones she liked and planned on using as inspiration for her paintings.

"Here," she said, stopping on one she'd taken of the courtyard. "I'm planning on painting it from this angle, because you get a nice view of the expanse of the courtyard without any of the pavement that's up near the top."

Ruby nodded as Taryn pointed. "I like that. Good thinking."

They grimaced in unison at the interior shots of the lobby, Ruby wrinkling her aristocratic nose and exhaling. "Not much to look at, is it?"

"Or smell," Taryn agreed.

"It always did have its own special brand of perfume." Ruby grinned. "Even back when we would go there."

Taryn desperately wanted to ask *why* they went there to start with but refrained. She didn't want to look like she was prying. Parker had lived in California, of course, and would've stayed someplace when he visited Nashville but there were so many other choices that would've been better.

Why didn't he just stay with you? she wanted to ask, but couldn't.

When they got to the pictures of Room #5, Taryn slowed down. "And here's the motel room. I tried to take it from as many angles as possible."

Taryn studied Ruby discreetly as she slowly scrolled through each picture, one by one. The other woman's face remained impassive, but her eyes turned glassy and a red sunburn rash began creeping up her neck. Taryn knew a woman attempting to hide her true emotions when she saw one. Although she was a sensitive person herself, she was good at hiding it in public and saving her own displays of emotion for private moments. She suspected that Ruby, someone in the limelight, had gotten good at doing the same.

When Ruby reached a shot of the bed, she stopped and brushed a stray strand of silver hair from her face. Her fingers shook, the only outward sign that she was troubled. Taryn, momentarily forgetting that she was sitting next to a celebrity, saw only the woman and reached out her hand.

"Are you okay?" she asked, gently touching Ruby's shoulder. It was thin and bony under her fingers, making Ruby feel frail. "Do you want me to put these up so that you can look at them in private?"

Ruby patted Taryn's hand, her fingers chilly against Taryn's own. "You're sweet," she murmured. "I'm alright, though. It's been a long time. I just hadn't seen the bed in so long."

"Is it the same furniture? I mean, as before?"

"No, not the same," Ruby answered. "The only original piece from our days is the mirror there on that wall by the bathroom. The rest has been added over the years. The bed, however, is in the same place. It *could* be the same one. It's in the same place," she repeated.

Taryn understood.

"When my fiancé died I eventually sold our place," she admitted. "Before I did, though, I tried living in it. The furniture brought back to many memories and I thought I might go insane so I put most of it in storage and bought new stuff. I thought it might help. The first night, though, I was sitting on the new couch in the living room and realized that even though it was a *new* couch, it was in the same position as the old one. I was still looking in the same direction, at the same view, that Andrew once had. I couldn't stand it. It was 3:00 am and I was up dragging furniture around by myself."

Ruby smiled unhappily. "Not many people understand that. Some want everything to stay the same. Others crave change. I go back and forth."

Taryn nodded. "So do I."

"It's been so *long*," Ruby grimaced. "So long. I shouldn't still be affected the way I am. Time is meant to heal, and in many ways it has, but there's an old hurt that just won't go away."

"Yes," Taryn agreed. "It's been years for me as well and yet sometimes it feels like yesterday. Other times it's almost like he was never here at all. It feels like a dream."

"Thank you for taking this job and for bringing the pictures to me," Ruby said. But Taryn could sense rather than hear disappointment in her voice and was concerned.

"Is everything okay? I mean, is there something else you wanted that I didn't get?"

Ruby rose to her feet and began pacing the room. She was surrounded by reminders of her success: numerous awards spanning her four decades in the business, framed candid shots of her with everyone from Dolly Parton to Bruce Springsteen, concert posters advertising her shows at places like Carnegie Hall and the Rose Bowl Stadium...

And yet now she had nothing but the look of a woman knee-deep in awful grief.

"No, you did a terrific job. The old place is an eyesore but the photographs are wonderful. You should consider doing an exhibit of your work. I have a friend who owns a small gallery in Franklin. I can talk to her if you'd like."

Taryn straightened with pride and folder her hands to keep from clapping with glee. "Well, yes, thank you. That would be nice."

Ruby stopped and turned, her skirt whipping around her slender legs. "I was wondering if you..." She let her voice trail off as her eyes drifted to the ceiling, searching for the right words.

"Yes?"

"Have you *seen* anything? I mean, have you felt or seen anything that's perhaps not...obvious?"

Taryn bit her lip and looked down at her feet. She noticed a clump of mud on one side of her left boot and hoped she didn't track anything into the house.

"I know the motel is meant to be haunted," she said slowly. "I watched some videos on You Tube of paranormal groups going in and investigating."

Ruby waved her hand, the large rings that adorned her fingers sparkling in the sunlight that streamed in through the bay windows. "Charlatans, most of them. EVPs and such. I never understood any of that. How do they know they're not just picking up on radio frequencies from other devices? And it's always the same thing. I don't trust those who make their videos and write their blog posts and do such things for publicity. I trust *you*."

Taryn, incredibly flattered, preened under her words. "I'm not a psychic," she said. "I don't communicate with the dead like some people claim to be able to do. Sometimes, though, I *do* pick up on stuff."

"Yes," Ruby said gravely. "I know."

Taryn wondered how *much* she knew.

"You do?"

"Yes, I do."

"I may have felt something in the room as I was leaving," Taryn said at last. "And maybe a few little things around the rest of the motel."

Ruby nodded in encouragement.

Now was the time to tell her about the picture, but she still wasn't sure she should. "How do *you* feel about these things?"

Ruby narrowed her eyes and pursed her lips. "I am not a religious person, but I am very spiritual. I am under no illusion that I will live forever and with each passing birthday I feel myself growing closer and closer to the end. The older I get, the more I feel connected to the things I can't see. Does that make sense?"

"Total sense," Taryn agreed. "I feel the same way, but mostly because I have a medical condition that affects me in a way that, well, let's say makes me feel closer to my own mortality."

"I'm very sorry to hear that," Ruby said, looking at Taryn with surprise. "You're so young!"

"It's okay," Taryn waved it off. "I'd like to hear more about what you were saying."

"Well, lately I've been thinking a lot about my past. I want to feel *connected* to it. In this business you're always moving forward, always thinking ahead. The stuff you did doesn't matter nearly as much as what you're going to do. You're only as good as your next album, next tour, next everything. I've spent a lot of time looking forward." Ruby paused and sighed, for the first time since Taryn met her looking her age. "I miss my friend. I miss Parker something fierce. But as hard as I try, I can't *find* him. They say that a person is never truly gone as long as they're in your heart but that's not true. I can't feel him at all!"

Taryn felt tears welling up in her eyes. She understood. She, too, had never felt Andrew. It was as though when he died he'd moved straight on to whatever was awaiting him, leaving nothing of himself behind in her world.

"I want to know that there is something else out there. I *need* to know that this isn't the end. I want to feel him again."

Taryn lowered her head. *Yep*, she thought, *I'll have to tell her.*

"Then there's a picture I kept back that you need to see," she said aloud.

Ruby walked back over and sat down by Taryn while she pulled up the image she'd left out, the one of the man by the door. When it popped up on the screen, Ruby gasped, a strangled noise that sounded like she might be on the verge of choking or crying.

Taryn watched, helpless, as the other woman's eyes filled with water that she held back. With a steady hand she reached towards the computer and gently outlined the figure, her coral-painted nails barely touching the screen.

"It's him," she whispered. "He's *there.*"

"Maybe," Taryn explained slowly. "He may not really be there. The room might just be remembering. Sometimes we, my camera and I, pick up on leftover energy. It doesn't necessarily mean his spirit is trapped in the room or that he's still there."

"But it could mean that," Ruby countered.

"It could," Taryn relented, not wanting to get her hopes up.

"I've been in there several times, trying to find him. I've called out to him, spoke his name. But he's never come to me," Ruby said softly. "He doesn't come to *me*."

"Miss Dixie is my conduit," Taryn gently explained. "She helps me with these things. I can't always pick up on them on my own. I don't think it's *you*. Sometimes these spirits have little control over what they can and cannot do."

"Taryn," Ruby said suddenly, turning to face her. "I haven't been honest with you."

"Oh?"

Ruby shook her head. "No. When I said I was familiar with your work, well, I didn't just mean your paintings. I also meant your work with the afterlife. I discovered you on a website about the paranormal. I read the newspaper articles about you and your work in Indiana and on Jekyll Island. I know this sounds like the ramblings of a crazy old woman, but I bought the motel because of *you*."

Taryn felt the blood draining from her face. "I don't understand," she whispered, confused.

"I want you to help me find my Parker. I want you to bring Black Raven Inn back to life so that he can return to me. *That's* why I hired you." The quiet desperation in her voice nearly broke Taryn's heart. "Can you help me?"

NINE

So *she wants you to help her find* the man she used to sing with?" Matt asked with his usual blend of skepticism and healthy dose of cerebral curiosity. "As in his ghost?"

Taryn rooted around in her plastic tub for her box of charcoals while she balanced her phone on her shoulder. "Well, he was more than that but basically, yeah. She thinks I can help and I'll be more discreet than a run-of-the-mill psychic or ghost hunter. She thinks I am a conduit to these things."

"Well, you *are...*" Matt pointed out.

Taryn shrugged. It wasn't really her that was the conduit, it was Miss Dixie. They were kind of a team.

"Anyway, she also gets a painting out of it from me so I guess her money goes further."

"And you're not going to run to a tabloid or anything," Matt agreed.

"Right."

Now that she was set up with her folding chair, charcoals, and sketch pad she made herself comfortable. The lobby was still dreary, but she thought her eyes were starting to adjust to the gloom.

"So what are you supposed to do if his ghost pays you a visit?" Matt teased her. "Tell him to stay right there while you call her and she hightails it over to the motel?"

Taryn laughed and then felt a little guilty. Well, it was kind of funny. "She's hoping I capture some things on film. I don't know that she actually wants to be here."

"So the one picture wasn't enough?"

"Not for some people." Taryn frowned. "When you've lost someone, you want as much of them as you can get. I told her I couldn't make any promises but that I'd do what I could. That means I'm going to have to spend an awful lot of time in that room."

"Taryn?" Matt's voice grew serious again, a sign he was putting a lot of thought into what he was about to say. "Are you sure this is good for you? Getting lost in the past like that again? Each time you do it, it takes a little more out of you..."

"Matt," Taryn replied with the same patience she once used when he was arguing the logic, or illogic, of her favorite Saturday morning cartoons as children. "This is what I am supposed to do. This is why I'm here. I don't always like it but running from it doesn't help. It just so happens that this is the first time I've actually been *paid* to do it."

"Okay," Matt said in return, but she didn't have to hear it in his voice to know he wasn't convinced; she could all but feel his hesitancy through the miles between them. "Just one more question."

"What?"

"How on earth are you going to make your paintings reflect the hotel in a positive light? I mean you're good but are you really that good?"

Taryn busted in laughter. The booming sound echoed through the dark, stuffy space until it was almost radiant.

IT *TOOK* Taryn more than three hours to sketch the lobby to her satisfaction. For now, her drawing represented the space as it was. Once she began painting she'd wave her magic wand and take it back to a better, gentler time when it was at least clean and new, if not sparkling and beautiful.

She planned on doing a lot of research to locate photographs of it from the 1950s and 1960s, although most of the work would stem from her own imagination.

Taryn had worked with a lot less; she'd recreated houses that been almost totally demolished in fires, without any pictures or original artwork to work from.

Matt was right, though. This was a challenge of a different kind. In the majority of her jobs, the structures she recreated had once been beautiful and stately, if not grand. The Black Raven Inn had never been beautiful by any stretch of the imagination. She could make it look authentic and true to its original construction, though. Perhaps slightly better without totally embellishing the design.

"You turning in for the day?" Aker asked in a tone that was casually polite, if not entirely friendly.

"Yep! It's getting late and my tummy is growling. You have a nice day?" She was bound and determined to win him over. Eventually.

"It was quiet. That's all I ask for," he replied with resolve.

Taryn imagined that he had seen a lot in his day; his present job must have been downright boring. Other than the rat (which he knew about) and the hand on her shoulder in Room #5 (which he *didn't* know about) nothing had caused any excitement in the time they'd been on the job. All he had to do was unlock the gates, search the perimeter and interior before she started work, and sit out in the sun all day while she did her thing. It wasn't exactly life on the beat.

"Let's start early again tomorrow, okay?" she asked as they began packing up their respective vehicles. "I need to catch that morning light so that I can see in there."

"Early is fine with me," he replied, adjusting his dark sunglasses and brushing a speck of invisible lint from his jacket.

"And, uh, by 'early' I mean—"

"Nothing before 10:00 am," he finished for her. "I know the drill."

Taryn grinned. In a weird way, it was almost like having a partner.

The pale moon was already sharing the sky with the sinking sun when Taryn drove back towards Hillsboro Village and her apartment. After a drive through White Castle, she took a turn down Music Row, blowing on her hot fries as she cruised past the signs congratulating songwriters on their latest hits.

"So depressing," she murmured.

She was saddened to see that so many of the bungalows and buildings that had once housed publishing companies and record labels were empty. Growing up, Music Row had been a thriving area, full of professional offices for the music business. Now, many of the companies had either closed or been bought up by larger companies or relocated to newer buildings closer to downtown. Some had moved to Los Angeles. The little shopping area off of Demonbruen that was once home to a Barbara Mandrell museum and George Jones gift shop was now a virtual ghost town. Even Shoney's was gone.

On the other hand, downtown was booming. As a child it was virtually empty. Her own grandmother had once remarked that you couldn't get her to "drive through downtown in the broad daylight." As a teenager, she'd watched as Second Avenue enjoyed a revival, what with the line dance craze and building of the Wild Horse Saloon and Hard Rock Café. Broadway, Second, and Printer's Alley weren't just places for liquor and live music—now you could hardly walk down any of them on a weekend without bumping into families with camera and toddlers in tow.

Taryn's own neighborhood in Hillsboro Village had seen its fair share of changes, too. When she'd first moved in the main draw had been a used bookstore and the Pancake

Pantry. The Pancake Pantry was the size of her living room back then, and the lines stretched around the block if you didn't know what time to go. Now there were more than two dozen boutiques and cafes. The old Belcourt Theatre had been revitalized and showed arthouse films, and the whole area was teeming with hipsters and industry professionals alike.

Ironically, the Pancake Pantry had expanded and was now three times larger than it had been—and the lines *still* wrapped around the building.

Things changed. Taryn wasn't really that keen on changes.

Although she'd spent most of her childhood in Franklin, Nashville was still her "hometown" but while she could appreciate the economic growth the city had seen, it no longer felt like *hers* anymore. She'd always kind of liked the grittiness and blue collar worker meets old southern money feel the city had kept. She liked the fact that she could go to the Green Hills Mall and walk through the shops with fur coats, pretending she had money, while still cruise Broadway and see struggling musicians standing on the street corners with their guitar cases open for change. Now there was a glossiness to all of it, a Hollywood finish that made it all feel like a replica of something else.

It was still her favorite city, though. It was hard to imagine living anywhere else.

As Taryn turned into her parking spot, she groaned with soreness. It had been a long day.

Her building was old and rambling. It creaked and moaned with every stiff breeze and there were smells inside that grew worse with each passing year. But from her bedroom window she could see the Nashville skyline with the Batman building's ears poking up and at night the lights of the city shone through and sprinkled her floors, making her feel less alone.

That part of Nashville was still hers.

Someone was playing the guitar outside. He could hear the music drift through the thick, rancid air and find its way into the cramped room where it wrapped itself around him. He was hot and sticky and the stench was making him sick to his stomach but the sound of the music was pure and

clean. *It cleansed him as it washed over him and, for a moment, he felt unsoiled and alive again.*

The moment ended when the musician stopped and the music abruptly departed, leaving him alone and empty again.

His legs jerked, rising briefly from the slick bedspread; he could feel the miniscule insects crawling over them even if he couldn't see them. In panic, he looked around the room, trying to find something heavy enough to place on them so that they'd stop twitching. He'd have given anything to have someone sit or lay on them—some kind of weight to keep them grounded.

Sweat rolled from his forehead in droplets that pooled under his neck. The pounding in his head was relentless. Moaning, he raked his hands through his wild hair and turned to his side, bringing his knees up to his stomach. A few years before he'd eaten some bad chicken and ended up in the hospital with salmonella. He was sicker than a dog and thought he might die.

This was worse.

While the pain and sickness were bad, though, his mind anguished him the most. Heart beating wildly, thoughts a jumbled mess, panic swelling in his stomach—he felt like that moment in a dream when you're falling and are just about to hit the bottom. Only the sensation never ended.

The phone on the nightstand next to him rang, the shrill sound filling the room and making his legs jump again. He looked at it and considered it but then closed his eyes. The mere thought of lifting the receiver, of talking into it, of trying to form a sentence... It was all too much.

He was a failure. A complete failure. His mother, before she hung herself in the bathroom on the day before his eighteenth birthday, had told him that he wouldn't amount to anything and she'd been right. He'd failed at everything he had tried. He couldn't handle the world, couldn't handle making decisions, couldn't handle living. It was all too much.

Even the thought of her, *with her decency and sweet smile and angelic voice was painful. She'd be sickened to see what he* really *was inside, to see what was happening to him. He'd fooled her, fooled everyone, for awhile. But this, him writhing on the bed with a puddle of vomit on the floor, was the real him. They'd all see that soon enough.*

He had to do something before they did.

TEN

Hurry it up, Aker, I'm losing daylight," Taryn snapped.

As he rounded the corner of the building and saw her standing with her hand on hip, tapping her foot impatiently, he paused and lowered his sunglasses. It was the first time Taryn had seen him without them. His eyes were piercing blue and startlingly unlined.

"I can do my job well or I can do it quickly," he said, steel lacing his voice.

"I'd rather you did it quickly," she grumbled but his continued gaze made her redden. "Sorry."

Ignoring her, he marched to his chair and plopped down without ceremony. "It's clear," he snapped, picking up his book.

She smirked at the true crime novel and then turned on her heel, sketch pad under her arm. As she trudged towards the hotel, though, she could feel her ears burning. It wasn't like her to be intentionally rude to someone, at least not to someone who didn't truly deserve it.

"It's the damn dream," she grumbled aloud as she turned the knob to Room #5. "It's thrown my whole day off."

She was already inside with the light on before she realized she'd forgotten her fold-up chair back in her car.

"Well, shit," she sulked.

Biting her lip, Taryn turned and peeked out the grimy window. From her vantage point, she could see Aker sitting in his chair. Although the book was open in his hands, even from where she stood she could tell that he was still alert.

"Like hell I'm going back out there again right now," she said, embarrassment still shaming her. She'd much rather do it the Magill way and return a respectable hour or two later—when she could pretend like nothing had happened.

The chair in the corner of the room had seen much better days, but it had a plastic seat so she could dust it off and not worry about bugs or critters that might live inside the cushions. She hated thinking about some of the things that might have happened on such a surface. Still, desperate times called for desperate measures so, using the hem of her Eagles' "Hell Freezes Over" tour T-shirt, she wiped away the dust and perched on the edge. When she was pretty sure it wasn't going to collapse underneath her, she opened her charcoal case and began laying out her tools on the bed in front of her.

"This feels weird," Taryn muttered, glancing up and taking in the sad-looking room. "Like I've been here before."

Of course, she had been there before; she'd visited the room several times already, taking her pictures, and had just been in it the night before in her sleep.

There'd been no question about where she was in her dream. She'd known right away that it was Room #5 that the figure on the bed who was her but also was *not* her was writhing around in pain in. The dream had been horribly unsettling and painful; she'd woken up drenched in her own sweat with the lower half of her body in so much agony, it had taken double her regular dose of pain medication and a hot bath in Epsom salts to get it under control again.

She hadn't felt right since.

Taryn knew it was Parker that she'd channeled in her sleep.

"No wonder the guy died of an overdose," she said now as she remembered. "If that's what withdrawal feels like I'm not surprised he couldn't stay clean."

She'd heard that withdrawal felt like the flu but what she'd experienced hadn't felt like any stomach bug she'd ever had. It had been a combination of mental and physical anguish so severe that even death had been desirable.

As unsettling as the dream had been, and as strong as her feelings were about addicts and self-medicating, especially when it was difficult for the people who needed pain medicine to get it, she still felt a soft place in her heart for the man she'd briefly "met." The desperation had been real enough, regardless as to whether it was caused by the drugs or by something else. He had been in more than just physical pain; he'd felt hopeless.

"This room certainly didn't help matters," Taryn muttered, taking a look around.

For its part, the room seemed to grow just a little bit smaller at her words.

Suddenly feeling claustrophobic and closed in, Taryn set her sketch pad aside and walked to the door. "Let's just let in some air, shall we?"

With the door propped open with an ancient rubber door stopper and fresh sunlight pouring in, she could breathe easier. The path of light only reached a few feet into the room but she could see it and coupled with the gentle breeze that found its way in she was reminded that there was still an outside world.

She wished Parker had been able to remember that, too.

"Okey dokey, let's get started." Taryn actually clapped her hands, a cheerful noise out of place in the bleakness, and began to draw.

TRUE *TO* her nature, two hours later she stopped for lunch and headed back outside where she plastered on a sunny smile and approached Aker.

"Hey," she called.

The man looked up, his expression unreadable. He appeared to be more than halfway through his book already. *Must be really boring sitting here by yourself, day after day*, she thought.

"Are you taking a break?" he asked.

"I was going to go out for lunch," she said.

"Okay, I'll lock up after you," he replied amicably.

"Actually, I was wondering if you'd like to go with me. My treat for being a bitch earlier." She shot him her most winning smile and hoped she looked both pleasant and remorseful.

Aker frowned. "I don't know. I was just going to run down to the sandwich shop."

"Well, I was feeling Thai food," she said, remembering that she'd seen him with a takeout carton from a nearby Thai place a few days before. "And I always eat by myself. It would be nice to have some company."

"I suppose it would be appropriate, considering the circumstances," he relented at last.

Taryn started to ask what the "circumstances" were but then shrugged it off. "Great! You want me to drive?"

"I've seen you drive," he replied. "I'll do it. Since you're buying and everything."

Since it was the closest thing the man had made to a joke since she'd been working with him, Taryn laughed. "I'll wait while you lock it all up then," she said.

The Thai restaurant was a ten-minute drive away but the minutes felt twice as long in the silence of the car. She was impressed by its cleanliness and general order and surprised by the Spanish guitar music that played softly on the radio.

"So how long you been doing the guard thing?" she asked.

"Eight years," he answered, not removing his eyes from the road.

"And before that?"

"Detective."

Well, so he wasn't a conversationalist, she thought. He surely had other attributes.

"Have you worked for Ruby Jane before?"

At first he hesitated, as though trying to decide if it would violate a confidentiality agreement, but then he must have decided it was a harmless enough question. "I travel with her on the road sometimes and provide security at her shows."

That was a subject Taryn couldn't drop, even after they were seated inside the small, crowded restaurant.

"So do the fans get wild at her shows? Do you have to, like, keep them off the stage or something?" She was trying to envision the fans at Ruby's concerts. All she could see were hipsters and middle-aged women. Maybe the occasional star-struck man who was trying not to show his adulation in front of his wife.

"You'd be surprised," Aker muttered. "Her fans are a different breed."

"What do you mean?"

Aker laid down his menu and studied Taryn from across the table. "I've worked with male entertainers, too. With them, you get the women. Women of all ages hanging out by the stage door, stalking the tour bus, screaming the performer's name, throwing notes with phone numbers on the stage..."

"Just typical concert stuff," Taryn interjected. She'd attended enough shows to know the drill.

"Yes, well, that's for the male entertainers and their female fans. When it comes to female artists and *their* fans, it's a different story," he said drily.

"Like what?" Taryn was fascinated. She didn't often get a behind-the-scenes look at the industry from an actual insider.

"The women want to be close to the men. It doesn't matter what the man looks like or how he acts. They want to be physical with him, as though being close in," Aker's face reddened, "in that nature will make them a part of the singer's life—if only for a moment. I see it all the time. They don't really want the singer, they want a piece of that charisma, a piece of that talent, a piece of that idolatry. They do it through being physical."

Taryn knew that was the truth. She'd seen women of all ages strutting their stuff around the stage, flirting with the roadies even.

"With the female performers, though, it's a different story. Their groupies are of a different breed," he continued.

Taryn stopped, her fork halfway to her mouth. "You mean there are male groupies for female singers?"

"Not men," he shook his head, "women."

That had her attention. "So there are women out there who try to sleep with their idols?"

Aker's face turned red again. Taryn was starting to enjoy that side perk of making him uncomfortable. "No," he said in a strangled voice. "The women don't, ah, want to be physical with the other women. But they still want a piece of them. They do that in a different way."

"Ooh, do tell!"

"Rather than trying to wear the revealing clothes and throw themselves at the singer in a sexual way, they go for their heads. They essentially try to make themselves the loyal best friend," he concluded.

Taryn sat back, wheels turning. "So you're saying that for female singers, the women groupies try to weasel their way in through friendship?"

Aker nodded. "It's all for the same outcome, and no less obvious or pre-meditated."

"So these women do what," Taryn asked. "They ask Ruby out for dinner, invite her over to their house?"

"Sometimes," he agreed. "And they tag her in photos of the two of them and call her by her first name, as though they were hanging out at a restaurant rather than at a backstage signing session. They send her Christmas cards and presents, inquire about the family, read up on intimate details of her life and then insert those details into the brief conversations they have with her as though she confided in them herself."

"But isn't it just kind of a country music thing to feel close to the artists we like?" Taryn asked. "I mean, I am a huge fan of George Strait. I know he's married to Norma, I know his son goes by 'Bubba.' And sometimes I do talk about him like he's a neighbor or a cousin. But I always thought that was because country fans feel a deep connection with the performers, something on a personal level."

"There's a difference, believe me," Aker grumbled. "You might refer to 'Cousin George' in conversation but have you ever sent him an invitation to your college graduation? Followed him from city to city and pushed your way to the front of the autograph line with the sole purpose of him becoming familiar with you? Because that's what this is about. These women, they want the artists to know them. It's as though because the entertainer is in the public eye, if they know the fan's name then the fan suddenly matters more— not just as a fan, but as a person."

"Geeze. That is weird."

"Ruby has one 'super fan' as we call them, who goes to all her shows, no matter where they are. She's convinced herself, and her followers on social media, that she and Ruby have a special relationship. You know what it's like on stage with all those lights? Ruby can't see more than a face here and there in the crowd. But this woman convinces everyone that not only does Ruby zero in on her face for each show and direct songs to her, and her alone, but that she's actually responsible for helping Ruby pick the set list and that Ruby is singing straight to her when she performs."

"And that's creepy."

Aker nodded in agreement.

Suddenly, Taryn felt a stab of sympathy for Ruby. *How can you ever know who is legit*, she asked herself silently. *Does she know who her real friends are? Does she have any real friends?*

Taryn's thoughts were interrupted by a commotion at the register. Aker was alerted as well and in an instant he was up on his feet, his body turned towards the front.

The small, friendly Thai owner who normally had a big smile and laughing eyes was plastered against the wall, a look of horror on his face.

A skinny man in dirty jeans and stringy hair who stood before him, waving a revolver, was shaking. "I'll give

144

you what I have," the owner cried, his voice shrill. The tables closest to the scene recoiled in fear, shock on their faces.

On instinct, Aker stepped in front of Taryn and reached his hand back to her. Without turning around, he let his hand rest on her shoulder. "Under the table," he snapped softly.

Taryn obeyed.

Before she knew what was happening. Aker had crossed the short distance of the room. From her view through the lace tablecloth she could see him swiftly disarm the shaky man with one swift movement of the leg. The revolver flew up into the air and then landed a few feet away, where a patron quickly grabbed for it and held it in front of him in disbelief.

Aker, with his arms locked in a grip around the man's waist, calmly turned to the rest of the room and said, "Someone called 911 yet?"

An hour later, as they walked towards his car, Aker cracked his knuckles and rubbed at his hands. It was the first sign of nervousness he'd shown.

"Hey," Taryn grinned, punching him lightly on the shoulder. "You were kind of a bad ass in there."

"I have my moments," he said thinly.

"You were like, gonna protect me and stuff," she teased him. "I think that's pretty cool. Admit it, you like me."

145

"I've worked with worse," he agreed.

But even with the dark glasses on, Taryn could tell that he was smiling.

ELEVEN

I worry," Matt said. "How do you get into these messes? Do they just find you or..."

"I don't exactly go out looking for this kind of nonsense," Taryn protested. "It just seems to find me."

"I wonder if you did something in the past that's turned the Universe away from your favor," Matt mused.

Taryn, feeling slightly offended, sulked. "Well gee, thanks."

"I just believe in karma, that's all. And you *do* seem to have more than your fair share of bad luck when it comes to people wanting to hurt you."

Taryn shrugged, even though he couldn't see her through the phone. Or maybe he *could*. "Well, in any case, Aker was there and he took care of business. Like a boss."

"I'm not sure I like you hanging around with a big, beefy, macho dude every day." Matt's tone was teasing but Taryn could hear a bit of worry mixed in there, too. Nobody would ever accuse Matt of being macho or beefy. Or big. He would fit in more with the cast of "The Big Bang Theory" than "The Walking Dead."

"Yeah, well, I don't think I could ever hook up with a dude who rations his humor and smiles," Taryn replied. "I'm not naturally funny myself. I need someone with a good sense of humor to balance me out."

"Like me?" The hopefulness in his voice reminded Taryn of when Matt was a little boy, seeking approval for a science project he was proud of when his own parents ignored him.

"Like you," she agreed.

"I'm going to come up in a few weeks. I have some time off. If I don't take it, they'll start complaining. There might even be a mutiny."

"Are you being hard on your students again?"

Matt grunted. "They deserve it. I mean, really. I was never that unmotivated and lazy as a college student. What's wrong with people these days? They do just as little as they can to get by."

"Well, dear, some of them have social lives. The reason you were able to give 110% was because you never left your dorm room unless it was for class, the library, or work study," Taryn teased him.

She could tease him about this, because she'd been the same way. Both were late bloomers as far as their social lives went; Taryn was thirty one and still waiting for hers to take off.

"*You're* my social life. I just save it all up and use it on you," he said with complete seriousness.

She believed him. Matt was all business and little play unless she was around and he'd always been that way. He divided his time between work, preparing for work, cooking, shopping for essentials, and watching television. He lived a short drive from the beach and only went when there was an employee function, unless Taryn was there.

"Speaking of visiting..." Taryn began slowly. She was in the middle of heating up a take-out carton of macaroni and cheese and paused with her hand on the microwave door. "I'm, er, getting company in a few days."

"Oh yeah? Who?"

"David."

She let the name hang in the air between them, the air thickening despite the distance between them.

"Hmmm..."

It wasn't that Matt disliked David necessarily–he was just jealous. As jealous as Matt could get, anyway. When she'd worked on Jekyll Island, David had been around quite a bit.

Matt, who'd considered himself her protector long before either one of them had known what it meant to date, much less acted on any feelings, had trouble with the idea of someone else acting as knight in shining armor. The fact that David was good looking, amiable, and shared common interests with Taryn didn't help. Had they met under other circumstances, they might have been friends. As it was, the two men could barely disguise their uncomfortable scrutiny of one another.

"He's coming to town for a lecture at Belmont and invited me to listen. I'm going to dinner with him after," she explained.

To avoid awkwardness, she'd considered not telling Matt at all. If she knew him, and she did, he'd worry needlessly and work himself up over nothing. While she flirted with the idea, Taryn knew it wasn't a real possibility. She'd never been good at hiding things from him, sometimes telling him more than he needed to know.

The almost-psychic connection between them would've had him knowing something was up before David was even on a flight back to Brunswick. Best to just be upfront and honest.

"Do you want me to come up while he's there?" Matt asked, sounding hopeful.

"Matt..."

"Yeah, yeah. Okay," Matt grumbled. "Fine. So how far along are you on this job anyway?"

By the time Taryn hung up, she was feeling newfound motivation. She was ready to sketch and paint, and as a vision of the courtyard flashed through her mind she was struck with inspiration. She knew *exactly* where she could stand to capture the essence of the enclosure and present it in a fun and unique fashion.

Unfortunately for Taryn, it was midnight. Aker might have been at her disposal, but she seriously doubted he'd have a sense of humor about meeting her in the middle of the night so that she could paint.

"Well," Taryn exhaled noisily. "Damn."

Resigned to the fact that she'd either have to ignore her muse and wait until the next morning, or work with what she had, she opened her laptop and began pulling up the photos she'd taken. With old school Reba playing softly on her CD player, her easel dragged out to the middle of the floor, and "Teen Witch" (a highly underrated 1980's teen movie) flickering on mute from her television set, she began to work.

Something hard and heavy collected in the courtyard, growing stronger and more powerful as the individual parts came together to form a bigger whole.

It darted around the enclosed space, sniffing the air and seeking something tangible to attach itself to. It slithered across the ground, leaving an invisible trail of foul-smelling slime in its wake like a thick, fat slug.

As it moved through the thick night, objects in its path were left to rot or decay; a soda can it slinked over all but melted under its weight, the tin left crackling. The paint on an overturned chair bubbled then slid off, leaving a puddle of dirty white on the hard ground.

When it reached Room #5, it clambered up the door and encircled the knob, the old metal glowing brilliantly hot and red under its touch. The door wobbled a little then swelled, filling its frame until it might explode and send shards of wood and metal across the courtyard. The essence quickly turned inwards on itself and darted inside through the keyhole.

There, it waited.

TARYN *HAD* felt productive and happy when she finally turned in at 6:15 am. Although she could see the dark red streaks of the sun rising over the downtown skyline, the sky was still navy blue and dark. When she'd pulled her blackout curtains to in her bedroom, she'd snuggled down into her blanket and had fallen to sleep like a baby. Taryn didn't like sleeping alone as she often suffered from nightmares, she didn't do well when it was totally dark (which is why she kept her door open and a lamp on in the living room) but she loved her sleep.

She knew before she even opened her eyes at noon that it was going to be a rough day.

Every bone in her body hurt. Her right hand was swollen to nearly twice its normal size. Her back was so stiff that it took three tries to sit up, and when she attempted to swing her legs over the side of the bed and stand, she immediately fell to the floor; her hips and legs couldn't support her weight.

The sharp, shooting pains that radiated from her hips and shot down to her feet had her eyes watering and her stomach turning. Somehow, she managed to make her way to the bathroom by holding onto furniture along the way. There, she collapsed on the floor on a throw rug and emptied her late-night binge of brownies and apple juice into the toilet. By the time she was finished, her body was burning with fire; sweat rolled down her face and back and her heart pummeled her chest.

She wouldn't be working today.

The walls, furniture, and doorframes supported her weight on the slow journey into the living room. From the couch, she made a call to Aker and apologized for the disruption of the schedule.

"Sorry, Aker," she said brightly into the receiver, trying to make her voice sound light and airy. "Must have stayed up too late last night and am feeling the effects this morning. I'm going to be working from home."

Her voice broke on the last word as another fiery bolt of pain streaked through her system. Aker did not let it go unnoticed.

"Don't worry about me," he replied, with what could've passed as gentleness in most people in his voice. "Do you need anything?"

"No, it's okay," she whispered, feeling embarrassed. "I just need to rest."

"I don't mind running out for anything," he said. "I need to pick up something from Wal-Greens for my mother."

Taryn allowed herself to briefly picture Aker's mother and imagine Aker as a devoted, loving son, before she replied. "I'm okay, I promise. I have medicine here. It will knock me out and this day will just be a nightmare."

"Take care then and let me know what you want to do about tomorrow."

When she hung up, Taryn turned on the television and found a true crime show on the Investigation Discovery channel. Her pain medication was within easy reach but when she tried standing again to go to the kitchen for a drink, she couldn't. By then, the pain from her waist down was excruciating. Taryn thought that if she had government secrets she'd talk.

A Coke she'd started fourteen hours earlier was on the coffee table in front of her. It was warm and flat, and a fly was trapped in the stickiness on the tab, but it was all she had. Grimacing, Taryn took a sip and swallowed the oval pill. It was bitter on her tongue. Before her, Rose was telling a St. Olaf story to a bored Blanche and Dorothy. The canned laughter from the audience filled her living room as the first strong rays of sunlight filtered through her curtains.

And Taryn cried in frustration and disappointment.

TWELVE

Two days. She'd lost two days.

"Dang it," Taryn muttered as she shoved her plastic tub into the backseat. The brushes and plastic palettes rattled around inside. Her wrapped canvases, which she was much gentler with, were stowed in the trunk next to a carton of Ale-8, mailed to her from Kentucky by her friend Melissa. She'd become addicted to the drink when she'd worked at Windwood Farm. Now Melissa was more or less her pusher, sending her a carton of the ginger-tasting drink once a month.

She was still achy. The extra pain medicine she'd taken had her head fuzzy, leaving her feeling hungover.

And now, of course, she was behind. She'd have to work extra hard over the next few days to play catch up with herself. She'd promised Ruby to bring the canvases by once she had something to show.

Taryn, someone who almost obsessively concerned about meeting deadlines and not wanting to let others down, would almost run herself into the ground to ensure she did what was expected of her.

Since she'd been put on the strong pain relieving medication she took great care in how she took it. She never, for instance, drove when it was freshly in her system. She didn't want to be responsible for a crash. So today, even though it hurt to walk (and stand and sit), she was flying high only an Epsom salt bath, a couple of Tylenol with some arthritis cream on her legs.

"Let's do this thing," she said, forcing some cheerfulness in her voice as she pulled away from her parking spot.

She *would* get back on track and *would* get this job completed.

THE *OUTSIDE* temperature was in the high seventies, nary a breeze wafted through the air, and there wasn't a cloud in the sky.

Room #5 was cold, almost bitterly so, and damp.

Taryn shrugged a cardigan around her shoulders and burrowed inside it, trying to generate extra body heat. The bright sunlight pouring in through the front door was impeding her view of the room so she'd closed the door. That had cost her whatever heat was coming in from the outside world, however.

Annoyed, Taryn rose from the chair and hobbled across the floor, wincing as her right hip popped and cracked along the way.

"Settle down," she muttered, slapping her jean-covered hip in reprimand. "Don't start crying yet. We're not finished."

Talking to herself, her various body parts, and the room in general kept her from feeling lonely.

With the door open, she could already feel the warmth seeping back in. Taryn stood in the doorway for a moment and opened her cardigan, allowing the fresh air and sunlight to wash over her.

The room's frosty air nipped at her back, chilling her. There was something else, too, something she couldn't put her finger on. It was also cold but in a different way. This other thing that poked at the back of her legs and skulked about her shoulders was unfriendly and moist; it left a dampness behind on the places it touched her.

Taryn shivered and, feeling violated, quickly turned around.

The motel room was empty.

She returned to her chair and straightened the towel she'd been sitting on but remained standing. "I'm not afraid of you," she declared to the room. "So if there's anything you want to do, you'd best be getting it out of your system right now."

The front door slammed closed with a "bang", the sound exploding in the tiny, confined space. The framed picture of Parker Brown fell from the nightstand, shattered glass scattering across the grimy floor. His radiant smile looked up at her through the cracks. He appeared almost angelic.

Taryn wrapped her arms tightly around herself and closed her eyes, willing her heartrate to slow down. Her instinct was to run screaming for Aker and make him check under the bed and in the closet, like any frightened child might have their parents do.

She envisioned herself running, or *limping* in her case, to him shouting, "Daddy! Daddy! There's a monster under my bed!"

She saw him rising from his folding chair, patiently placing his book down (after carefully marking it with the "Friends of Police" bookmark), and striding with purpose to the room– his dark sunglasses and impassive expression hiding any urgency on his part. And then she saw him on all fours, lifting the soiled bed skirt and searching for her monsters.

The idea did the trick; Taryn's fear slowly subsided and the beating of her heart steadied under her trembling hand. She even felt the tickle of a smile on her lips.

"That wasn't very nice," she said, ignoring the tremor in her voice.

Marching back to the door, she opened it once again, flinging it open wide until it hit the wall behind it. Once again, the room filled with fresh air and sunlight.

Taryn then turned and painfully crouched down to pick up the shards of glass that littered the floor. She placed

Parker's picture back in the cheap wooden frame, sans glass, and returned it to the nightstand. She kept her fingers on it, however, and studied the image.

Once again his beatific smile radiated outwards, the demons he possessed unrecognizable in the 1960's publicity shot. Taryn paused to admire the Nudie Suit he wore, the sparkle of the rhinestones nearly as brilliant as the gleam in his eyes. The piercingly white color of the suit stood out from the stark, beige desert setting in stunning contrast. His long hair fell softly to his shoulders, his smile serene and gentle.

She hoped he wasn't trapped in the room, hoped that he'd somehow made it out.

The door banged closed again, this time with a force so strong that her easel tumbled to the ground, sending her canvas with it.

Parker's picture flew from her fingertips and soared across the room, hitting the wall on the other side of the bed before it dropped to the floor with a thud.

Shaking, Taryn closed her eyes and took long, deep breaths. There was nothing she wanted more at that moment than to pack it all up and leave. She wasn't even sure she could make herself move, however; fear was a crippling thing.

"Ghosts can't hurt you, ghosts can't hurt," she chanted almost silently to herself.

If there was one thing Taryn had learned through her adventures, it was that she had more to fear from the living than the dead.

She hoped that was still true.

THIRTEEN

Taryn *stood in the courtyard*, Miss Dixie in hand, and waited. She'd meant to work on the lobby that day but something had called to her from the courtyard. She had done a preliminary sketch of it but hadn't started painting yet. Now, she was ready.

Headphones on, she turned to an Emmylou Harris CD. The soft, lilting voice was a gentle contrast to the bleakness of the inhospitable surroundings before her. The soothing sounds of the music reminded Taryn that her position was temporary, that there were still beautiful things in the world.

She needed that when meth-making materials were within her line of vision, the empty bleach bottle with its top cut off gathering dirt beside one of the rooms.

Even though she'd already taken several dozen pictures of the space already, Miss Dixie had itched to be taken along. Taryn never ignored her camera's pleas. Now, she lifted her to her eyes and focused on the center of the enclosure, taking in as much as she could.

When she turned on the playback, the scene before her changed.

The rickety picnic tables, painted a faded redwood color and stained with cigarette scars and things Taryn didn't want to think about, were replaced with white stone benches and patio furniture. Colorful umbrellas rose from the circular tables, their flaps gently moving in an invisible breeze.

Where a pile of garbage decayed next to a cheap grill turned over on its side was in present day, a brick fire pit glowed with a hearty flames. Chairs were pulled up around it and next to one of them was a worn guitar resting on its case. The dents in it reminded Taryn of Willie Nelson's beloved "Trigger."

Several leafy trees, all gone today, offered shade. The stone patio was smooth and clean and swept of debris– in contrast to its modern counterpart that was fractured with weeds growing through the cracks and strewn with soda cans and fast food wrappers.

She knew it was impossible (well, the whole *thing* was impossible but that was beside the point) but even the sky looked bluer.

For a moment Taryn was totally transported to another time period, a different lifetime. While she hadn't captured any people in her shot, she could totally envision the place being a crash pad for the struggling musicians of the time. She could see them, not through Miss Dixie but in her imagination, hanging out in the courtyard, visiting with the other guests, barbecuing or playing their instruments. It would have been an inexpensive place to stay back then, still popular with long-term guests and probably still drawing those who dipped into drug activity and were facing demons (like Parker) but it would've been cleaner back then–better maintained.

It wasn't the cesspool of filth and despair it would eventually become.

Back in the present day world, Emmylou sang about missing someone and feeling regretful that she couldn't remember if they'd said goodbye the last time she saw them.

People were confused as to why Ruby Jane wanted to buy the motel but Taryn wasn't. Part of her had even wanted the remains of the car Andrew had crashed. In fact, she'd returned to the scene of the accident almost a year later and gone for a walk along the side of the road at sunset.

The area had long been cleaned and processed; the vehicle and the fiery mess it had left behind were long gone. Still, as she walked back to her own car her shoe had kicked something that didn't sound or feel like a rock. It rolled a good three feet and when she knelt down to study it, she found herself holding a knob from the radio dial. She'd known it was Andrew's because it was faded and worn from the way he'd hold onto it; incessantly rubbing his thumb over it while he was driving was one of his nervous habits.

Taryn had placed the knob in her pocket, resumed the walk to her car, and treated herself to frozen yogurt.

Later, back in her new apartment, she'd removed the knob and set it on an antique mirror she'd put on her dresser to use to catch jewelry.

Buying the motel that contained the last place that saw her partner and loved one alive? Taryn got that.

People did strange things when they grieved–just about anything to feel close to them again.

HER *PAINTING* was calling.

Taryn had tossed and turned all night, too tired to sleep. She'd spent forty-eight solid hours working on the courtyard canvas without any sleep. Wired for the first time in a long time, Taryn felt totally focused and dedicated. Nothing was distracting her. She'd worked at the motel, barely stopping for a lunch break, and had gone straight back to her apartment where she'd continued without even turning on the television.

Her body was tired but her mind was still running on "high." She'd made herself go to bed, knowing she needed sleep, but she couldn't turn her brain off. It was jumping all over the place, landing on random thoughts and worries.

Her hands itched to pick up a paintbrush; the feeling was so intense she could all but *feel* the weight of the brush in her hand. It was almost painful.

"How long can a person go without sleep?" she texted Matt and then sat up. She'd taken Benadryl and it hadn't even phased her. Melatonin hadn't done a thing.

She just needed to work.

The canvas, still up in the middle of her living room floor, was ready to go. Taryn staggered to it and, with what was akin to nervous energy, opened her tubes of paint and began mixing. The scene before her was alive with life and color. It was starting to look realistic enough that one might think they could walk right into it.

Taryn picked up her brush and began dabbing gray onto the patio, swirling it and blending it until she could almost see the individual grains of the gritty cement. She painted the guitar resting on its case, the cheerful fire emerging from its pit, chairs grouped together for a late-afternoon jam session, guitar picks in a Mason jar on a patio table. In the background you could see the freshly-painted doors leading into the rooms off the courtyard, their brass numbers polished and gleaming in the muted sunlight. A few of the doors were cracked open, invitations to join the inhabitants or perhaps a sign that the guest was already outside with everyone else.

It was a cheerful, laid-back scene and Taryn worked feverishly on it, barely stopping to catch her breath. Gone were the dripping air conditioners, the rubbish, and the desolate landscape of a lonesome place. It was replaced with a scene just about anyone would want to walk into and relax.

Taryn worked until her hands were swollen, until her tummy rumbled from hunger.

Had she eaten yesterday? She stopped, brush in midair, and considered. She didn't think she had.

Sweat poured down her face, soaking her night shirt. Her underarms smelled. Her curly red hair frizzed and hung down her bang in a tangled mess from lack of brush and washing. Her legs hurt from standing.

The sunlight on her feet was warm and Taryn turned, surprised. It was already daylight; she'd worked through the night. Glancing at her phone had her startled—it was 9:30 am. She was meant to be at the motel in half an hour.

Taryn quickly rinsed her brushes and gathered her materials for the day. She didn't have time to hop in the shower, so using a washcloth she took a "hooker's bath" and smeared on some chap stick. After giving her jeans from the day before a glance over, she decided they were clean enough and slid them on. A George Strait "Check Yes or No" T-shirt hung limply on her chest, a reminder she'd lost weight, and an old man's cardigan would keep the chill off.

She was ready for a new day.

FOURTEEN

"ou don't look well," Aker said as soon as Taryn stepped out of the car.

"I didn't sleep well last night."

"It shows," he replied drily.

Despite the lack of sleep, Taryn was still wired, almost manic. The urge to continue painting was strong in her. She was being incredibly productive which, while not unusual, was still odd considering how poorly she'd felt only days before.

"Listen, I'm going to work in the courtyard today," she said.

Aker nodded, already heading to the lobby. "Still going to check everything out," he called over his shoulder.

"Yeah, yeah. I know the drill."

She was finished unloading her car by the time he returned. He was frowning, however, and Taryn paused, her the bag holding her canvas slung over her shoulder. "What's up?"

Aker's face was hard to read behind the stoic expression and big sunglasses but she was good at reading body language; something was clearly wrong.

"Someone's been here," he replied.

"They mess anything up?"

Aker shrugged. "Not exactly. They just moved some things around. Nothing looks like it's missing."

Taryn produced a thin smile at the thought. "Yeah, well, it's not like there was much to take..."

"I have learned that people will steal just about anything. Give them a chance and they'll lift a roll of toilet paper," he muttered.

"Everything look okay, though?"

One of the few things that scared her was being in the wrong place at the wrong time. Lord knew that happened to her enough. With the Black Raven Inn, in particular, she was concerned about stumbling upon a drug deal or something else she had no business being at. She'd read the motel's reviews about it being a hot spot for hookers, dealers, and pimps and even though it was closed old habits died hard. She didn't want anyone feeling homesick and thinking they needed to return for sentimentality's sake.

"Looks like someone just went through everything in the lobby and Parker's old room," Aker shrugged. "Maybe just a fan. That happens sometimes. It's like they don't care he died more than thirty years ago–they still think they're going to find one of his cigarettes or something."

"Do you think that whole thing's weird?" Taryn asked, setting her tub on the ground. It was getting heavy. "I mean, the people who came here to stay in his room and make little shrines to him? A lot of them weren't even alive when he died."

"I don't find much of anything strange anymore," he answered. "I've been at this job for a long time. Just look at the number of people who visit Graceland. A lot of them were not around in Elvis' lifetime but they still pay their money to play looky-loo in the Jungle Room, file past his grave in somber silence, and walk through the Lisa Marie."

He had her there; Taryn had also visited Graceland and done those exact same things. She hadn't felt weird about it at the time.

Still, Parker's fans actually visited the motel, stayed in a place where a dead body once laid in the parking lot for twenty-four hours without anyone noticing, and slept on the same bed in the same place where their idol accidentally committed suicide. That was more than a little morbid to her.

"Guess I'll be going to the courtyard," she said at last.

"Give a yell if you see or hear anything that's not meant to be there," Aker advised, settling into his chair. He had a new book today, a biography on Patty Hearst.

"Will do."

Taryn let herself in through the side door that would take her straight to the courtyard. It was a little bit of a shock, seeing it in present day after spending all evening and all night seeing it in the past.

"Do you need something from me?" She'd been working almost nonstop. Ruby wanted her to make contact with Parker's ghost, but Taryn didn't know how to do that. She'd never really intentionally tried to see a ghost before, only hoped they came out.

She didn't know what she was doing. All she could do was paint.

"If you're here, can you give me another sign? I don't know what to do," she complained. "I don't know what I'm doing."

Taryn set her supplies on the ground, put her easel together, and began getting out her paints. She was already starting to get lost in the work again, when something tugged at the ponytail that hung down the middle of her back.

It wasn't a physical tug, not like someone was standing behind her, but more like a reflexive jerk that had her straightening to attention and looking around. The tiny hairs on the back of her arm stood straight up as a creepy crawling sensation started at the small of her back and worked its way to the nape of her neck.

She shivered in the warm morning light and looked around. She was alone of course, but couldn't shake the feeling that someone was watching her.

With the satisfaction that Aker was on the other side of the wall, ready to spring into action, Taryn began a slow walk around the perimeter. He was right, someone *had* been there; she could feel it. It was the sensation that she got upon entering a small room just seconds after someone else had left it. She could almost still sense their presence, still feel the disrupted molecules and shift in the air.

Just moments before she'd arrived they'd stood in that very spot, the one she was standing in now, and had looked around at all the motel doors the way she was doing. Their feet had been firmly planted in the same ground, they'd breathed in the same pocket of air. Taryn closed her eyes and inhaled–she could almost taste their scent. A combination of musk and something floral, with just the slightest hint of a bitter undertone.

Miss Dixie was hanging around her neck, a little beat up from Jekyll Island but still working as well as she ever did, and Taryn turned her on now and aimed her at the space before her. Nothing unusual appeared in the shot.

When she made a 180-degree turn, however, and aimed her camera at the distance between her and Room #5 she startled at the results.

The motel room was open in her picture where, in present day, it was closed. A puff of smoke from a cigarette, hidden by the wall, lazily emerged from the room. One lone boot tip protruded from the bottom of the doorway, the rest of its owner concealed in the shadows.

Taryn took a step forward and took another shot, zooming in on the door.

The photo came back without anything unusual setting it apart from the hundreds of others she'd taken at the motel. The door was closed.

Still, it had meant something. She knew that.

As Taryn drew nearer to the door, the sensation of the invisible thing crawling up her back returned, this time even stronger. She stopped and turned and found herself facing the little shrine a few feet from the door.

It was still faded and messy from the elements. The ceramic angel with the vacant eyes was missing a wing; the gazing ball was cracked down the middle. A film had settled over the candles, guitar picks, and stone crosses. Letters were soggy messages and bleached by the sun until they were unreadable.

In the middle of the mess, however, was a Celtic cross. It stood upright when most everything else had been knocked over by wind and neglect. Its color had been untouched by the sun or rain. It was still a brilliant shade of jade.

As Taryn knelt down beside the shrine and peered at the fixture, the tiny words scrawled across the bottom caught her attention.

"'May the sun shine warm upon your face," she quietly read aloud, the carving blazing brighter with each word of the traditional Irish prayer she read.

"Until we meet again." The soft words were whispered gravely in her ear, the seductiveness not lost on her. The hot breath on her neck was sweet and tasted faintly of wine. She could almost feel the touch of lips on her clammy skin, their heat and suppleness spreading a warmth through her body that wasn't unwelcome. The other body that encircled her was invisible but she could feel both its strength and fragility engulfing her. Closing her eyes, she could see strong hands resting on knees on either side of her—the long, pale fingers gentle. If she leaned back just a little she thought she might feel the heat on her back.

Taryn wasn't scared. It occurred to her that she should be, but she wasn't. In fact, she was a little aroused.

Seconds later the presence was gone and she was once again alone, just a single woman stooping before a cluttered shrine to a minor star whose light had ceased to shine long before she was born—a name that would almost certainly mean nothing to the newest generation.

Taryn stood and shivered; without warning, dark clouds had inked out the sun and a breeze was stirring. A Happy Meal box blew past her and danced around the shrine, coming to land next to an empty, cut-out bleach bottle. The juxtaposition of childhood innocence next to what she could only assume to be drug paraphernalia kicked her in the gut.

She shook her head.

In a moment of lucidity and break from the manic it became clear to Taryn that she'd need to be careful with this job. It wasn't like the others she'd had. This one might be dangerous to her in a completely different way.

As she walked back to her easel, feeling jittery from the nervous energy that built inside her, one thing was for sure, she was certain that she'd been led to the shrine on purpose.

Someone had been there recently, someone who had left the cross for Parker.

"Someone with something heavy on their mind," Taryn whispered aloud.

The courtyard did not reply.

On Taryn's iPod, Emmylou sang about crying a river for a man, a river that was too deep and wide for her to ever swim across.

TARYN *SAT* in her living room, her phone in hand, and tried to process the news she'd received earlier.

The phone call had been from her doctor. Well, not from her doctor, but from her doctor's *office*. She hadn't even heard from the physician herself, but from the scheduling clerk.

Her primary care doctor would no longer be managing her pain. Instead, she'd been referred to a pain management specialist; a doctor whom, upon Taryn's quick internet research, received scathing reviews with phrases like "wouldn't send my dog to him" jumping out and not exactly instilling confidence in her.

"The doctor will get you through the rest of the month," the scheduling clerk had informed her, "but, after that, you should be in with Dr. Hanan. Is that okay?"

Is that okay? What was Taryn supposed to say to that?

No?

Because no, that was *not* okay. Her doctor had not mentioned that to Taryn on her last visit, had not warned her in any way that she'd be dropping that aspect of Taryn's care. This news had come totally out of the blue.

"I don't understand," Taryn had told the clerk in a whisper. "Why is she sending me to someone else?"

"I'm not sure," came the clipped reply. "You'll need to talk to her about it yourself."

Taryn, who had the doctor's cell phone number in cases of emergency, had sent her a text. That was four hours ago. She hadn't heard anything in return.

It was silly, of course, but Taryn felt rejected. She felt as though she'd done something wrong and now Dr. Culver didn't want her.

Her parents were gone, her grandmother was gone, her fiancé was gone, and now not even her doctor wanted her.

"But I've done everything *right*," she insisted to her belongings. "I've been a model patient. I always take my medicine on time. I keep a pain journal. I've never broken our contract, always let her know when I'm hospitalized, have never asked for an early prescription... The only time I haven't had any drugs in my system during a test was when I had the flu and kept throwing them up."

The inconsiderate room remained silent.

She loved her doctor, trusted her. She'd been with her since her parents died. Her doctor knew more about her than anyone, outside of Matt.

When she was twelve, Matt had joined the Science Club. For the first time in probably *ever* he had friends outside of Taryn—boys who shared interests with him. One day Matt had called her after school, full of exciting news.

"We've decided that after we graduate we're going to buy a big boat and sail around the world, solving mysteries like the Loch Ness Monster and the Bermuda Triangle," he'd boasted.

Taryn, who was just starting to really feel the stirrings of interest for the opposite sex, had felt a tug she didn't fully understand. She just knew that she *had* to be on that boat, too.

"Can I come, too?" She'd asked it with confidence, certain he wouldn't leave her behind.

"Sorry," he'd replied instead. "All the positions have been filled."

It was silly, but she'd hung up the phone and cried.

She remembered that moment now and cried again, although she couldn't be entirely certain what the tears were for.

FIFTEEN

Matt had told her that a person could only safely go about five days without sleep.

Taryn was working on her fourth.

She'd finished the courtyard canvas the night before. It was back at home, safely drying on an easel in the corner of her cramped living room, the past gazing out in harsh judgement at her modern discount warehouse sofa and flea market rocking chair.

She'd meant to work on the lobby today. She was going to do it and then the hotel's exterior, leaving Room #5 for last.

That had been *her* plan; the Black Raven Inn had another one in mind.

Now, Taryn found herself entering the cold, damp motel room again, balancing supplies on her hip with a towel slung over her arm. She needed something to spread onto the chair. No way was her bottom going to sit there without a protective covering between it and the surface of anything in that room.

It was a typical late autumn day, a forecast of the winter days to come. The sky was colorless, casting a chalky white film over everything. Muted sunlight was filtered through a thick layer of clouds, doing little to add light or warmth. Taryn wore jeans, thick boot socks, old cowboy boots, a flannel shirt, and a man's cardigan she'd picked up from Goodwill. (She had a collection of them.) Too physically exhausted to do anything about her matted, oily hair she'd plaited it in a braid that hung down her back and topped it off with a newsboys' cap.

She wasn't sure how she was moving at that point, much less driving. Her whole body felt like it was full of molasses. If she stayed in one spot for very long, she was afraid she'd become rooted to it.

And yet, her mind wouldn't stop.

She'd replayed the whisper and sensation of the man behind at her the shrine over and over in her mind so many times that she'd actually made herself physically ill. She'd worried so much about things she had zero control over (the environment, the stock market, terrorist attacks abroad, the price of gas...) that she'd thrown up not once but three times.

Taryn could *not* shut off her brain.

"Is this house people on Adderall feel? Is *this* what it's like to have ADHD?" she asked the room.

If it knew the answer, it wasn't talking.

"What the heck's the matter with me?" she demanded, wearily removing her collapsible easel from its case and setting it up in front of the chair.

The room didn't have an answer for that, either.

Once she had all her supplies set up, from a bag Taryn removed the two spotlights she'd picked up at Target. Ruby had asked her to send her the bill but Taryn decided that wasn't necessary. She worked in dark, isolated places a lot. She might need them again. These, she put on the bureau and one of the nightstands. She plugged them into long, industrial extension cords and ran the cords outside to an outlet in the wall. The building's power was on—it just didn't work in that particular room.

"Of course," Taryn muttered to herself. "Because this room is *special*."

When she stepped back inside, Taryn shuttered at the chill in the air. "How is it possible that it's colder in *here* than it is out *there*?"

It was, too. The motel room had to be at least ten degrees colder than the sixty-two degrees it was outside.

"And how it is that sixty degrees in the spring feels so much warmer than sixty degrees in the summer and fall?"

She was full of questions today. She really needed to sleep.

Taryn felt bad for Aker. Keeping an eye on things basically meant keeping an eye on *her* so he had to continue sitting in the parking lot where the motel room's door was in his line of vision. She'd tried to talk him into at least sitting in his car, where the wind would be off him, but he'd declined. Instead, he'd brought a portable heater and generator and was parked back in his chair, thermos of coffee in one hand and a book (something about the OJ Simpson trial) in the other.

"I'm fine," he'd barked, annoyed by her concern and pestering. "Weather doesn't bother me. Part of my training."

Yeah well, Taryn thought, *it might have been "part of his training" but he was no longer a spring chicken.*

But he was a grown man, and could do what he wanted. She wouldn't argue with him.

The lack of sleep was making it difficult for her to eat, or keep anything down when she did manage to eat. For the past three days she'd lived on soft cheese and crackers and the occasional cup of tomato soup. Her tummy rumbled now as thoughts of pasta and cheeseburgers danced through her head. They were immediately replaced by a wave of nausea.

"Let's do this," she sang, settling into the uncomfortable chair and focusing on the scene before her. If anything, the lack of sleep and gnawing hunger were making her mind more alert and focused. She figured that must be why people fasted.

Still, she'd be glad when it was over.

THE *KNOCK* on the door startled her. The hand working a delicate floral pattern on the bedspread quivered, sending a line of red paint towards the ceiling on her canvas.

When Aker let himself in, Taryn gazed at him with glassy eyes, trying to focus.

Why is he *here*, she thought with agitation. *What was* he *doing in her room?*

She couldn't see the glasses or the black jacket hiding his muscular frame. Instead, she was looking at a head of shockingly blond hair, lively indigo eyes, and a thin body clothed in jeans and a paisley-patterned western shirt.

"Why are you here?" she asked, disconcerted.

The paintbrush in her hand continued to tremble, sending flecks of red paint across the canvas. Taryn either ignored them or didn't see them; she was focused on the figure in front of her.

"It's after 3:00 pm," the voice answered. "You've been in here since 9, almost six hours. When you didn't come out for a bathroom break or lunch..."

The voice drifted off and Taryn became aware of the fact that he was studying her, drinking her in.

"Taryn," it began gently, "when's the last time you ate? Slept?"

The figure moved towards her then and she flinched, dropping the brush.

"Whoa, whoa! It's okay, it's okay." He took a step back towards the door and stuffed his hands in his pockets. "I just needed to check on you."

The room began vibrating, a small sound that grew bigger by the second, until a dull roar erupted around them.

Aker held his hand against the grimy wall, confused. "What the hell is that?" he demanded.

Parker's picture fell off the nightstand again and landed on Aker's foot. The television trembled and Taryn watched through film that covered her eyes as another long crack emerged and slowly worked its way across the screen. The ceiling fan overhead began turning, kicking up the stale air and dispensing it around the room until both Aker and Taryn were coughing.

A jumble of voices began then, filling the room with laughter and life. They were men and while she couldn't make out a single man's voice, or tell what they were saying, the sound built up around Taryn and Aker until it enveloped them. It seemingly came from everywhere at once–from under the bed, inside the bathroom, outside the windows, and even from Taryn's plastic tub.

The sound was cheerful on the outside, but it felt superficial. There was an undertone of desperation in the voices, as though something unfriendly lurked beneath the words. Even in her confusion it was clear to Taryn something much more threatening was being implied.

She was afraid, afraid of the menacing undercurrent, afraid of the rumbling around her, and even afraid of Aker's presence. The fear that built up inside of her was completely unjustified but she felt threatened nonetheless. The urge to leave, to run, was strong.

She was rising to her feet, spilling the paint tubes resting on her lap, when it all came to an abrupt stop.

Taryn shook her head and closed her eyes. When she opened them, Aker was standing by the door, looking around the room in bewilderment. His jacket was open and, for the first time, she noticed a gun at his side. His hand was resting on it now, ready to spring into action.

Gone was the man with the blond hair and western shirt. Gone was the breeze from the ceiling fan. Gone were the voices and growling. They'd all been replaced by the familiar. Though Taryn's confusion and exhaustion remained.

"You need to go home and get some rest," Aker said gently, refusing to let his voice show the horror etched on his face. "You didn't even know who I was."

"I know," Taryn agreed softly, looking down at her paint covered hands. "But I can't sleep. I've tried."

"Let me help you pack up," he said.

He walked towards her with uncertainty, but Taryn didn't flinch this time. Instead, she remained still, helplessly staring at her hands.

"Huh. Well." Aker was gazing down at her painting, his brow creased.

"What?"

Taryn looked up then, and saw her painting. When her hand shook, the paintbrush had danced. Now, the bed, ceiling, and parts of the floor were splattered with crimson.

By accident, she'd inadvertently created the scene of a grisly murder.

SIXTEEN

*S*omething was in her living room.

Taryn had been watching it from the corner of her eye all morning. With the heavy rainfall and thunderstorm warning, she and Aker had decided not to chance the motel. Instead, she was working from home. Or rather, she was *meant* to be working from home.

It was hard to concentrate when a shadowy figure from her small hallway continued to move back and forth in her line of vision.

She hadn't seen it in all its glory yet, but she knew it was there. Every time she'd return to her canvas and get to working, she'd see it move and flit from one side of the hall to the other, moving at a lightning-fast speed.

It unnerved her to know that someone else was in the apartment room with her, for sure, but it was more annoying that it was playing with her.

"Leave me alone," she called out. The *thing* flew around the room so quickly it left nothing but a black blur behind.

Taryn jumped, surprised, and stepped backwards. The bar that separated her kitchen from her living room slammed into her back. She could already feel the bruise starting to form.

Room #5 gazed at her from its canvas, an echo of a place trapped in time—a place that hadn't existed in reality for decades.

Taryn took a tentative step forward, intent on returning to her work, but the five-foot long snake coiled around the leg of her easel had her stopping in her tracks. The serpent's coil reached her knees and the rattler was pointed straight up, undulating from side to side in a seductive warning. The snake turned its triangular head to face her as its tongue darted out in an ominous "hssss".

Taryn screamed, her earsplitting cry filling the room with terror.

The snake disappeared then, as though it had never existed. And perhaps it hadn't.

Leaving her painting where it rested, Taryn ran to her sofa where she collapsed and buried herself in a mountain of blankets, their softness and weight a comfort. The shadowy figure dashed from the hallway again, deliberately distracting her from her security.

No matter where she looked, something was watching her. She was too tired to drive, too exhausted to leave the apartment. Helpless, she pulled one of the Sherpa blankets up over her head and closed her eyes. At least if something was there she couldn't see it.

A crash came from her bedroom; something had fallen from her chest of drawers or dresser. Taryn jumped and then cursed herself.

"Mind over matter," she whispered. "Mind over matter."

With a resounding clatter, a painting she'd done of an old barn and had framed for her grandmother's birthday came hurtling down from its position over her console table, sending a porcelain fairy to the ground where it exploded.

It broke her heart to know that something she'd loved was broken, the fairy had been a present from Andrew, but still, she kept her head covered.

The creak of footsteps on the old wooden floors was just inches behind her. Whatever was in the room was standing next to her and the couch. Taryn held her breath and listened as it walked back and forth along the length of the couch, pausing at each end before turning around to go back in the other direction.

She was beyond scared, she was terrified. She wasn't sure she could move if she wanted to. The fear that ate at her was all consuming, rendering her paralyzed.

Now the creak of footsteps was on the other side of the couch, stalking her from the front. She listened to each footstep, flinching when something hard brushed against her protruding foot. She wanted to lower the blanket and look upon the figure intent on driving her insane but she was too afraid. Instead, Taryn reached into her pocket and drew out her phone.

"Matt," she whispered as soon as he answered. "Matt, I'm in trouble."

"What's wrong," he asked in alarm. "What do you need? Do I need to call the police?"

"No, but there's something here with me. It won't go away," she whispered again. "It's standing right here next to me."

"What is it?"

"I don't know," she replied, her eyes filling with tears.

It was slowly backing off and moving away. She could hear the footsteps growing fainter and fainter as it marched towards the hallway and then into her bedroom.

"I couldn't stop seeing things. There was something everywhere I looked, every five seconds. So I got on the couch and covered my eyes and my head but that's when the noises started," Taryn cried. "I don't know what to do. I'm so tired but I can't sleep. I'm hungry but I can't eat. And this *thing*. It won't leave me alone."

"Is it gone now?" he asked gently.

"Yes, as soon as I started talking."

"Taryn, you need to get some sleep. You could be hallucinating."

Taryn wiped her nose on her T-shirt and sniffed. "But it seems so real."

"Well, it *is* real in a sense. Your mind can do some crazy stuff."

"I've been trying to sleep but I can't."

Matt groaned, a sound of frustration from him. "You should talk to your doctor."

"Maybe..."

"Do you want me to come up there and stay with you for a few days?"

Yes, Taryn thought to herself. *Yes I do*. But she was too proud to ask.

"I'll be okay. I'll talk to my doctor. Maybe I am just exhausted."

"I'll come if you want me to. But if you don't get some sleep tonight then I'm coming up there anyway," Matt warned.

"Okay," Taryn replied, feeling a stirring of hope. Sometimes Matt did treat her like she couldn't handle things on her own, and that got old, but it was true that she needed him more often than she didn't. And vice versa. She'd have been down there in a heartbeat if something was happening to him.

"Matt," she lowered her voice again, afraid of what she was about to say. "I don't think Parker died the way they said he did. I think he was murdered."

"How do you know?"

"I saw it in my painting," she whispered. "I think that's why he's still there, still in the motel. I believe he wants me to help him, to help him find out what happened and get him to move on."

"Taryn," Matt's voice was alarmed. "I think you need to leave. I don't think you should go back. Please come down here and stay with me..."

"No." Taryn shook her head. "I can't let him down. He needs me."

"When are you meeting David? When's his thing?"

"Tonight," she answered. "I'm supposed to meet him at 6:00 pm and then we're going to dinner. I might take a cab over there to the college. I'm too tired to drive."

"I think that's a good idea."

The conversation trailed off then, as both of them became lost in their own thoughts and worries. By the time Taryn hung up the phone she was experiencing some relief, a reprieve for half an hour in which nothing popped out of the shadows or things flew from the wall.

IT *WAS* exhausting, but somehow Taryn had managed to wash her hair and even style it. Simply raising her arms in the air to work the shampoo in had been enough to nearly have her collapsing but now that it was dry and looked good, she felt better. She'd also thrown on a long-sleeved, light wool dress and applied makeup. It was a far cry from the jeans and hat she'd been wearing as a uniform every day for the past week. Looking good physically made her feel good mentally, even if it was superficial.

The parking spots around the college were all full so she had to park on Music Row and walk. It was a nice night, though, almost balmy. The rain had cleared the air and now everything smelled fresh and new, even though they were downtown.

She'd hoped to catch David before his presentation but she was moving slower than she liked these days and it had taken her longer to get moving than it normally did. He'd already been introduced and was walking towards the platform when she entered the ballroom.

As Taryn suspected, it was full of college-aged girls watching the front of the room with rapturous attention. The young men scattered throughout the folding chairs set up for the event didn't look that much less enchanted.

For over an hour the audience listened to David talk about Jekyll Island and St. Simon's and some of the research he and his team were doing there. He shared slides of the graves they'd discovered, talked about methodology, and even held up artifacts uncovered through their efforts. He spoke of Native American heritage on the island, the history of its settlers, and even mentioned the pirates.

The true story of Jekyll Island couldn't have been given better treatment by a Hollywood screenplay writer.

Of course, if they'd known what had happened to *her* on the island, it really would've rocked their world.

Nearly thirty minutes of questioning followed his session and then, when it was over, Taryn had to wait while he patiently talked to those who came up to ask personal questions and fawn over him. Taryn remained in her chair, a trashy romance novel open in her lap, while she waited.

"So was I that bad?"

David towered above her, more than 6-feet tall, and smiled down at her.

"Huh?"

"The book," he gestured. "Did you read it the whole time I was up there, or just during the boring parts?"

Taryn laughed. "Just using it to pass the time with. Your lecture was great. I learned some things and I already knew about most of it!"

"Yeah, well, I try to make it interesting for people. If they knew how much of my job was just sitting in the dirt with a brush or data entry they'd be much less impressed," he said.

"Hungry?"

"Starving. Let's go."

SEVENTEEN

So, *how are the islands?*" Taryn asked once they were settled into a booth and given menus. "Are they surviving without me?"

"Nah, not at all." David grinned.

"I didn't think they would. I figured I brought a little extra something to them."

"Well, I have to say, they're a lot more boring without you there," he admitted.

"Aw, David, are you having trouble making friends?" she teased him.

He shrugged, a glimmer in his eye. "You broke my heart when you left me, red. Now I just and cry in the dirt all day."

Taryn laughed and returned to her menu.

Once they'd ordered, David turned sideways in the booth and leaned back. "I figure I'll be another ten months or so. Then I'll go on to Arizona. If my house is still there, that is."

"You miss it?"

"A little," he shrugged. "But I don't mind being on the road."

"Me too," Taryn said. "The traveling part is fun. Granted, not as much fun as it was when I was in my early twenties, but I still enjoy it. Sometimes I just like to come back, look at all my stuff, and make sure everything is still here. Then I hit the road again."

"Are things a little better now since the hotel companies, you know..."

"Paid me off?" Taryn finished with a grin.

"Yeah."

"Well, the good thing is that I don't have to worry about work at the moment. I am now able to take the jobs I like and can be picky about them. In the past, I pretty much had to accept whatever came my way. So that's better."

"What are you going to do when..." David let his voice trail off and blushed.

"You mean all of this isn't going to last forever? No, seriously, I know what you're asking. And I don't know. I honestly don't know how much longer my health is going to allow me to do some of it, especially the traveling. It's getting harder and harder to ride in the car."

"Can they not do surgery for any of that?" he asked.

"They can," Taryn nodded and took a sip of her drink. "But they don't like to. Surgery is risky for people with EDS and they try not to do it unless there's an emergency. It's harder for us to heal, sometimes the surgery doesn't work at all, and they can actually do more damage because of the fragility of our tissue. Then there's the scar tissue that forms."

"So it's just pain medication?"

"Yep. That and water-based physical therapy. I do that at least once a year now. That's all insurance will pay."

"Damn."

"So what's after this for you?" Taryn asked.

"Don't know yet. I've been asked to teach for a semester or two at a university in Vermont. I might do that. It would just be adjunct, and I couldn't commit to it until I get this book finished, but it would be different and I'm up for something new."

"Speaking of Vermont...I'm about to hire contractors to work on my aunt's house in New Hampshire."

David slapped the table with enthusiasm. "Now you're talking! What are they going to do first?"

If there was anything Taryn and David loved most, it was old houses. There weren't many they didn't like. When Taryn's aunt, Sarah, had passed away she'd left Taryn the big, rambling farm house up in New Hampshire. It was in disrepair, however, and in need of a ton of work. Taryn estimated that it would take about a year, and a bucket of money, to get it set right again but she was up for the challenge. She couldn't just let it sit there and rot.

"I'm going to have the roof set, first," she said. "There are some pretty big gaps in it and I'm trying to avoid more water damage. I want to save the floors. Replacing them would be a real pain."

"Good idea," David agreed. "What next?"

"It needs an overhaul of the electrical and plumbing systems. That's the biggest expense so I need to get started on them. I was thinking I might even go up there in a few months and hang out, watch the work as it's being done. The whole house could use a good cleaning and I need to decide what can stay and what would be donated."

Although, in truth, she couldn't think about getting rid of any of her aunt's stuff. It had been her home, after all, and all that was left of her. As a child, Taryn had been closer to her aunt than either one of her parents. The idea of one of the greatest, and most interesting, women she'd known being reduced to nothing more than old furniture and pots and pans hurt Taryn's heart. She was going to hold onto as much as she could.

"Is Matt going with you when you go?"

"Well," Taryn blushed. "I actually haven't said anything to him about it yet."

"Hmmm."

Matt didn't understand Taryn's love for old houses or her desire to hang onto her aunt's house. He'd never been close to anyone in his family. Taryn was the closest thing he had to family, even though both of his parents were still alive. She also knew he couldn't take that much time off. It would drive him crazy to be that far away from work for that long again.

"I just think this is something I need to do on my own. For Sarah. For me," she added.

"I get that," David said. "You have a spiritual connection with her and with the property. Didn't you say that when you were a kid you always felt at home there? Like you were meant to be there?"

"Yeah and I also said I always felt like someone was watching me," she said.

"Maybe your spirit guide lives in the woods around the house," David suggested.

Taryn laughed and dug into her steaming plate of lamb.

"Hey, you never know. They have to live *somewhere*."

Taryn watched David in envy throughout the rest of the meal as he finished his lamb's meat, a salad, and a plate of baklava. She'd barely managed more than a few bites of hers.

"Look, don't take this the wrong way, but you're not looking too well," David said with concern once their plates were cleared. "You hardly ate enough to keep a fly alive."

"I haven't felt well lately. If I tell you something, will you promise not to laugh?"

"Sure."

Taryn proceeded to tell him about the motel, what had happened in the room with Aker, the snake, the noises in her apartment, and about the feeling of being watched. David listened with full attention and, as she spoke, Taryn watched the concern on his face deepen.

When she was finished, he sat back and studied her. "Taryn, when's the last time you slept?"

"This will be the fifth night," she answered softly.

"Jesus! You're going to kill yourself. You've got to get some sleep."

"You think I'm hallucinating? Matt said that," she muttered.

"Look," David said as he reached out and took her hand. "Whether you're hallucinating or not doesn't matter.

The fact is, you could be making things worse with the lack of sleep. If this is some paranormal thing after you, you're letting your guard down by not getting rest. You're lowering your defenses. Maybe that's what it wants."

"I've tried everything to sleep," she said, tears brimming in her eyes. "Everything!"

"Here, let me take you home. No funny business. I'll sit on the couch, you can talk to me about this some more, and we'll try to figure this out. I promise," he swore.

Taryn nodded and started to stand. When she rose to her feet, however, her legs buckled and she nearly tumbled to the ground, face first, in the restaurant.

"Whoa there," David said, wrapping his arm around her waist to hold her up. "There you go."

He helped her through the door but when they got outside he picked her up, like she didn't weigh a thing, and proceeded to carry her to his car.

"People are going to think you slipped me something and now you're toting me off to do vile things to me," she joked weakly.

"Maybe next time, lovely."

Somehow, she managed to direct him to her apartment.

EIGHTEEN

I'll *really be fine,"* Taryn *swore* as David plodded up the stairs to her apartment. "I promise."

"What? And keep me from the chance of carrying a pretty lady up the stairs and playing hero? Why would you take that away from me?"

"Well, here, at least set me down so that I can find my keys," Taryn muttered, embarrassed. As soon as her feet touched the ground, she swayed. Her legs felt like jello.

"Don't worry, I got them," he said as he reached his hand into her tiny backpack and fished them out. "I heard them rattling around earlier."

Taryn was thankful her apartment was mostly clean. She hadn't been expecting visitors but at least she didn't have dirty dishes piled up in the sink. Or, worse, dirty underwear piled up in the bathroom.

David led her to her sofa where she plopped down and stretched her legs out on the cushions. He locked the apartment door then chose the rocking chair next to her. "Nice place," he remarked, looking around as he took in the room.

"You can nose around if you want," she said, Taryn closed her eyes, waiting for inevitable ruckus to start. It didn't. Just like when she had Matt on the phone, the apartment was as quiet and aloof as it ever was.

"Don't mind if I do."

She could hear David walking around her living room and dining area, pausing at certain shelves and tables as he took in her belongings. "I like what you did here," he called from the dining room. "The shadow box with the shoe and dress?"

"I found those in an old house I was, er, exploring awhile back," she replied. "They were up in an attic. Just gathering dust and rat poop. I brought them, soaked them in vinegar, and then bought that shadow box to put them in."

"Nice."

"Yeah, well, the house actually burned down a few weeks later so I'm glad I rescued something."

"The shells?"

She knew he was referring to the old-fashioned pitcher she had filled with sea shells and pretty stones. "They're from beaches I've visited. There's some from Jekyll, St. Simon's, Daytona, St. Petersburg, Kennebunkport in Maine, Salem, and San Diego. I don't normally buy souvenirs but I like having something to bring back with me."

"I collect stones myself, and leaves. I press the leaves in a journal I keep," David offered as he moved on to a bookshelf.

"Have you written anything about me in that journal?"

"Maybe." He grinned. "Maybe it's all about you and how I'm pining away for my unrequited love."

"Oh please," Taryn snorted, but she laughed just the same.

"You've got, uh, quite the collection of books here."

"You should see my bedroom—and I don't mean that as a come on. Seriously, I can't stop with the books. I buy one just about every time I'm out."

"I hear you on that," he agreed. "But you're kind of all over the place. 'Ethan Frome' next to Nora Roberts. 'Gone with the Wind,' 'Great Expectations,' 'War and Peace', and V.C. Andrews?"

"I like variety." Taryn shrugged.

"'Misery,' Peter Straub's 'Ghost Story,' and," David paused then laughed, "oh, come on. This can't be a real book. 'Pride and Prejudice and *Zombies*'?"

"It is a real book and it's very good." Taryn sniffed. "It's just like the real one, except every once in awhile a zombie pops out of the woods and they have to attack him."

"I've heard everything now," he murmured, walking back to where she was sitting. "Move your feet over."

Taryn obliged and he sat down next to her, just inches away. She was aware of his presence, would have been aware even if her eyes had been closed. David emitted an energy that was strong and powerful. There was almost something otherworldly about it. Taryn was drawn to him in a way that made her increasingly uncomfortable, especially considering Matt was in the picture, and yet she was as relaxed around David as if she'd known him her entire life.

"Tell me some more about this motel you're working at," David prodded, patting her on the foot. "Anything going on there you want to talk about?"

"Well, it turns out that Ruby hired me to see ghosts," Taryn replied, closing her eyes again. "That's a first."

"She wants you to find her dead partner?" he asked with sympathy.

"You figured that out?"

"It made sense. Never underestimate sentimentality and what it can do to a rational mind," David reasoned.

"She's had physics and ghost hunters out there but I reckon they didn't give her the answers she wanted," Taryn explained.

"I don't trust many of those myself. The people who walk around with their little EVP machines and blinking lights, listening to the 'voices' coming through the static and asking their questions... And the ones who take pictures and see 'orbs' in everything? I worry." David shook his head, his coal black hair catching the soft glow of light from the lamp and glistening in the shadowy room.

"Hey, a lot of those are real!" Taryn exclaimed, feeling defensive. Since discovering Miss Dixie's talents she'd spent a lot of time perusing paranormal websites and forums, learning about different ways of contacting the spirit world and the various degrees of communicating with the dead.

"Some of them are," David agreed, "but you really have to question those who don't have a healthy sense of cynicism and skepticism."

"What do you mean?"

"If you're looking for something, and 100% sure it exists, then you're almost always going to find it—whether you've actually found it or not. You'll see what you're looking for in most anything. I went to high school with girls like that. They were convinced there was a soulmate for everyone, even though that's statistically possible. For everyone to have a soulmate, we'd have to have an equal number of people in the world and they'd have to match up fairly well by age. But I digress," he laughed, showing off his fine set of snowy white teeth.

David got up and walked into Taryn's kitchen where he found apple juice in her refrigerator. As he poured himself a glass, he raised his voice so that she could still hear him. "They believed in love and soulmates so much that they were always falling in love, always convinced that this new person was their soul mate. If they'd just stopped for a moment and looked at their situation, it would've been painfully clear to them that even if such a thing did exist, it wasn't the person they were with. Logically, what were the odds of that one girl's spiritual soulmate actually being in their hometown, in their class, at their school, etc.?"

Taryn laughed, in spite of herself. "Okay, I get your point. I went to school with those girls, too. But does that *really* apply to ghosts?"

"Sure it does. You believe in ghosts, you believe in orbs. You believe that orbs can show up in pictures. You take a picture, there's a ball of light in it, and—bam!" He clapped his hands together. "There's your orb!"

"Maybe it was an orb," Taryn suggested.

"Maybe it was. Or maybe it was dust, a reflection of the light, or any number of things. I'm a scientist. I believe in a healthy dose of skepticism."

"So what about EVPs?"

"What about them?"

"Do you think they're *real*?"

David pursed his lips and cocked his head to the side. "Do I believe that the dead can communicate with us? Unquestionable. I'm sure it's difficult for them, but I think it can be done. For those who whip out those little tape recording gadgets and ask all those questions, though, *that's* another story."

"I've seen people on investigations, though, and it *does* look and sound like the spirits are answering them back when they talk," Taryn protested.

"Those things can also pick up interference," David rationalized.

Taryn scoffed, a little put out by his logic. She got enough of *that* from Matt.

"Look," David began again, this time with a gentleness in his voice. "If you turn one of them on and leave it running, you're going to hear sounds. That's inevitable. You'll hear pops and cracks and moans and you might even hear voices that are carried through white noise. The human ear is incredibly adept at picking up patterns in sound—it's one of the main reasons we're able to speak and carry on conversations in the first place. It's why some people are so proficient at learning new languages—they're not especially good at remembering the words and learning the nuances of the language itself, they're just skilled at recognizing and learning the patterns."

Taryn listened, forgetting that she was originally miffed and now fascinated with what he was saying.

David, now that he was warmed up to the topic, grew more animated. Taryn watched in fascination as his eyes lit up and his body straightened. He began using his hands to describe what he was saying and to make his points. "Turn it on and ask it a question. You'll get a 'response.' Turn it on and *don't* ask it a question. You'll *still* get something in reply, the same thing you probably would've gotten if you had asked it something. It might come immediately or it may come thirty seconds later. Whenever it comes, we put meaning in the response. Ever noticed how what it's saying doesn't always sound like what the guy doing the investigation *says* it's saying?"

Taryn nodded. She *had* noticed that. She had gone on a paranormal investigation with a ghost hunter once and he'd insisted the ghost was calling him out by name. His name was "Stewart." To Taryn, the "ghost" sounded like it was saying "windmill." Stewart had been so proud of the development and his communication skills, however, that Taryn had simply gone along with him when he'd asked if she'd heard it. She certainly wasn't going to be the one to tell him the truth.

"You're on an investigation of an old railroad–the site of a crash one hundred years ago. The guy asks the spirit when it died, the 'spirit' responds with something that sounds like gibberish to you, and the guy gets excited and says, 'See! He says he died in 1889! That's the year of the railroad crash. He *must* have been on the train!'"

The tips of Taryn's ears warmed and turned bright red. Now she felt silly. She wasn't going to call it a "win" for David just yet, though.

"But you *do* believe in the paranormal," Taryn insisted. "I *know* you do. And you've seen my pictures and stuff. Do you think I am looking for things that aren't there?"

"No, sweetie," David replied, shaking his head and squeezing her foot. He left his hand there, the passionate heat from his fingers seeping through her sock to warm her toes. "I know you're the real deal. Ruby Jane can probably sense that, too. That's probably why she sought you out in the first place. That's why she trusted you enough to tell you the truth."

"Then why doubt what others have seen and heard? Is it because you don't know them?"

"I don't always 'doubt'. I *question*. My job is to investigate, and I do. That's all. I don't jump to conclusions right away; I look at the varying answers and then investigate until I can make an informed decision. I know there are lots of things out there I can't explain and sometimes the supernatural *is* the answer. But I also understand that it's not the *only* answer."

"The thing you said about girls in high school, and how it's crazy to think their soul mate ended up in their school, in their town and all?"

Taryn was embarrassed to even bring it up but David had, after all, started it.

"Yes?"

"I went to school with Matt. We met in elementary school. And he's *my* soul mate," she blurted out, feeling silly and childish.

"Of course he is," David said soothingly as he reached over and brushed a lock of her hair out of her face. "There are also different degrees of soul mates too, though."

"What do you mean?"

"Just because he's your soul mate doesn't mean you're meant to have a romantic relationship. Or meant to be together forever. Sometimes it just means that you're meant to find each other, that you travel through lives together. Just because you're meant to be together in *eternity* doesn't mean you're meant to be together in this life, on this earth."

Taryn felt chilled to the bone. What he said summed up one of the thoughts that traveled through her mind on a daily basis. What if she and David were soul mates but *weren't* meant to be together in this life? What if he was just one of many she was supposed to find, like her grandmother and Aunt Sarah?

What would she do if he wasn't *the one*? It would rock the entire core of her foundation; Matt was the only rock-steady thing she had. Without him, she would lose her footing and everything around her would crumble—of this she was sure. It had happened before.

There *was* something else she needed to get off her chest, though.

"This motel I'm working at, there's something there," Taryn said with hesitation. "I don't want you to think that just because I've worked at haunted places in the past I think there are ghosts everywhere, but there *is* something at this one."

"If you say there is, then I believe you. Has the old gal picked up on anything," he asked, gesturing towards Miss Dixie in her spot on the coffee table.

"Yes, a few things. And I've heard and seen things myself."

She quickly gave him a rundown on what had happened so far and David listened, giving her his full, undivided attention. When she finished, he tapped a little rhythm on her foot with his fingers as he gazed across her living room and contemplated her story. The casual movement was done casually, like a habit, and it provided an extraordinary intimacy between them that Taryn found disconcerting.

"Well," he said at last, "in the time I've known you I have found that these things don't generally find you and communicate with you unless there's a reason. Am I off base here?"

"No. They *do* seem to have an agenda."

"Then it would seem to me that whatever this is in need of something," David said. "He or she or *it* desires something from you. The fact that it followed you home is different, of course. This apartment has nothing to do with the Black Raven Inn, Parker Brown, or Ruby Jane."

"That we know of anyway," Taryn pointed out.

"Right; that we *know* of."

"The thing that was in my apartment today, that didn't feel like Parker. He was a gentle soul. Everyone said that."

David gave her a questioning look.

"Okay, so I've done some research on him since getting this job," Taryn confessed. "A lot. And David, I think he was murdered. I don't think he died the way they said he did."

"I wouldn't jump to conclusions and assume that this entity must be Parker, though. That motel has been around for a long time," David said. "Parker is its most famous resident, of course, but there were others. Hell, doesn't the old motel sign say something like, 'Stay where the legends stayed'?"

"Yeah. Of course, they weren't legends when they stayed there–they were down-on-their-luck singers who were looking for a break so that they wouldn't have to hock their instruments." Taryn stopped and then looked down at the floor. "Parker was clean at the end. I don't think he would've gone back to that stuff he was doing. And even I feel weird after working there. Maybe there *is* something to the motel."

David's face paled to an ashy chalk; she could almost hear the wheels turning inside his head. Whatever he was thinking, however, he remained vague. "Who knows what else has happened in it. Please be careful. You don't know what you're dealing with here. You be sure to stay with that bodyguard of yours. I have a feeling about this one. I don't think it's going to go well."

"Ghosts can't hurt me," Taryn whispered, unexpectedly seized with a slow burn of dread that scraped at her stomach and throat, burning both. "They *can't*."

"What if it's not a ghost?" David asked, his face engraved with concern. "I'd worry about this, Taryn. I worry about *you*. Haven't you noticed that with each job you get, things get harder; the division between you and that other world gets weaker?"

Taryn bowed her head. She had.

"At what point does it just become too much? What's your breaking point?"

Taryn didn't know. But there were days when it felt awfully close.

WHEN *SHE* opened her eyes, Taryn was in her bed. The duvet was pleasantly cool against her bare legs and the soft cotton of her favorite T-shirt laid against her chest.

She sat up and looked around, confused at the late-afternoon sunlight that smiled dimly through her blackout curtains. When she reached for her phone, she found it on mute.

She didn't remember going to bed. She didn't remember removing her dress, although now she saw it folded gently over the back of an antique chair in the corner of her bedroom. She didn't remember putting on the T-shirt or undressing at all. When she felt her chest, however, she was pleased to find that she was still wearing her bra.

So she hadn't gotten completely naked in front of David. That was good. And she was wearing underwear that covered her entire bottom, not one of the little slutty pair that she sometimes wore for kicks.

The socks she'd been wearing were across the room in the hamper by the door. She could see them from the bed.

Her jewelry, including her grandmother's ring, was in a little glass dish on her nightstand.

So sometime during the night she'd gotten undressed, put on her favorite T-shirt, folded up her dress, put things in the dirty clothes, shut her curtains, removed her jewelry, and muted her phone. And she didn't remember any of that.

Frightening.

A glance at her phone told her that it was 4:30 pm.

"Oh my God!" Taryn shrieked, jumping to her feet. She had missed a whole day's worth of work. And Aker would've waited on her. She hoped he hadn't waited long.

After throwing on her robe, which had somehow made it to the foot of her bed from the hook behind the bathroom door, Taryn darted into the kitchen.

"Caffeine. Coke," she chanted. "Must have Coke."

A handwritten note on the refrigerator door had her coming to a halt.

Dear Taryn,

You drifted off last night and I didn't want to wake you. It seems like all you needed was my foot-rubbing talent! Ha! Anyway, don't get mad but once I knew you were out for good I took you to your room and tried to make you comfortable. I know it probably sounds weird now, but once I found a T-shirt I thought felt soft I closed

223

the curtains and the room got pretty dark. I promise I didn't peek or cop any (unnecessary) feels. I stayed on the couch so there wasn't any funny business.

It's a little after noon now and I am getting ready to leave to catch my flight. I called your body guard and we both agreed you needed the rest. I turned off your phone so that you could get rest, in case any telemarketers or bill collectors called (not implying that you don't pay your credit cards on time, of course). I hope you sleep for awhile. You were looking pretty comfortable when I left. I checked on you throughout the night to make sure everything was okay.

If you need anything, please ask. You know I'll be there in a heartbeat.

Love,
David

NINETEEN

Taryn *was amazed at how much good* a whole night's rest was. Her mind was calmer than it had been in days and even her body pain was somewhere at a manageable level.

She took a good, long look at the painting she'd done of the courtyard and barely remembered working on it.

"What the hell happened to me?" she asked herself, shaking her head. She didn't know, but she didn't want it happening again.

Her phone buzzed, an email notification, and she walked over to her computer to check it out.

"Can meet at the Parthenon in twenty minutes," the message read.

Taryn glanced at her watch and moaned. It would take that long for her to drive there. Still, it might be the only chance for her to meet with Griff Townsend, former night manager of the Black Raven Inn.

After quickly typing back a reply, Taryn ran a brush through her hair and then pulled a newsboy cap snugly down to her ears.

She didn't have time to do much else and was soon on the road towards the expansive lawn that surrounded one of Nashville's most popular landmarks.

The Parthenon was built to scale and while perhaps not as awe-inspiring as the original of the same name, still pretty interesting. It was popular for couples on picnics, families who wanted to let the little ones run around, and college kids playing a game of football.

When Taryn pulled up and parked, she was happy to see that it wasn't as crowded as it could be.

She didn't have any trouble recognizing Griff; he looked pretty much as his message said he would. The man who ambled towards her was tall and reedy. The long beard that nearly reached his waist might have been ridiculous on the thirty-year old's lean body ten years ago, but now beards and flannel shirts (the "lumberjack look" Taryn called it) were back in style again.

"Griff, I hope," Taryn grinned after waving him over.

"At your service," he replied.

He had a bit of a deep northeastern accent that made Taryn wonder how he'd found himself all the way to Nashville, much less a desk worker at a seedy motel.

"I was hoping we might be able to sit down a bit," she said.

He nodded and Taryn began leading him the way to the cement steps at the foot of the towering replica of the Greek monument. From their seats they had a view of the entire park. Only mothers with young children were out at the moment. Taryn figured everyone else was either working or trying to sleep off the night before.

"So you're wanting information about the old motel," he ventured.

"Yeah," Taryn replied. "I have a few questions about it. You're the only one I could get in touch with."

"Not surprised," he said. "Most of the other guys have gone on to greener pastures. Some on the other side of the great holy river, if you know what I'm saying."

Taryn nodded.

"I'm particularly interested in Parker Brown's death," she began.

Griff laughed. "Of course you are. They all are."

Taryn decided to ignore that quip and forge ahead.

"I was wondering if you heard anything about his death, anything that sounded odd. Like maybe," she paused for a moment to collect her thoughts. "Like maybe he didn't do it."

"You think he was killed?"

"Well," she replied, feeling lame at the suggestion. "Maybe."

"Ma'am, with all due respect, nobody can force you to take drugs. Talented as the guy might have been, he was chasing the dragon just like the rest of them," he snorted.

"Chasing the–"

"Chasing the dragon," he finished for her. "Means trying to keep the high going, trying to recreate that first-time feeling. Lots of 'em do it, few succeed."

"I know he died before you were born, just like me, but wondered if you'd heard any stories."

"Like what?"

"Like how he was found, what he'd been doing earlier that evening, if he was dead on arrival," she answered. "Things like that."

"Found by a woman," Griff replied. "They called her a girlfriend. She supposedly wasn't with him at the time of the overdose but came later. Called the cops and front desk and then left. Nobody talked to her. She just kind of vanished into thin air."

"A woman?"

"Yeah, said she was his girlfriend. Truth be told, I think she was probably more of a hanger on. You know what I mean?"

Taryn shook her head no.

"Happens a lot. Men and women both like to cling to these celebrities, get as much as they can from them, and then move on when the well dries up." Griff shrugged. "That's what it sounded like to me. A real friend woulda stayed around, you know?"

Taryn said she did. "Anything else?"

"I always heard that if they'd been called sooner he would've lived. That time was wasted, especially if he had somebody with him."

The thought pained Taryn greatly. To know a tragedy could have been prevented was awful. Poor Ruby.

Unless...unless Ruby had been the "girlfriend" there with him.

"One more thing," Taryn said as she watched the young mothers slowly pushing the strollers around the walk paths. It was a beautiful day; the sun was shining high in the sky. She was glad to be out in it.

"Shoot."

"I know a lot of paranormal investigators and people were there over the years. Did you ever hear or see anything in the motel, and especially in Parker's old room?"

Griff snorted and lowered his head, shielding his eyes from hers. "Ma'am," he said at last. "You couldn't pay me to go inside that room. Lots of good housekeepers felt the same way."

"Yeah, why?"

Griff shook his head then visibly shuddered. "There's something about that whole place that's just not good. Me? I used to be a pretty happy guy, pretty optimistic. Came down here to a studio musician. I play lead guitar, you know."

Taryn smiled encouragingly.

"After three months in that place I started losing all focus. Barely wanted to get up in the morning, much less play. After three years I wanted to slit my wrists. Still trying to work out some of the inner demons I picked up there."

"Why didn't you just leave? Why'd you stick around?"

Griff winced. "Cause something like that, it gets under your skin. Makes you think there is nothing else out there, that life just ain't worth living. Makes you think it's all you have."

Now it was Taryn's time to shudder.

"I gotta tell you this, though," he added. He looked up and stared at Taryn with green, watery eyes. "If you're in there now then my advice is to get out and get out fast. Have you started losing sleep yet?"

Taryn nodded. Griff appeared troubled.

"Then it might just be too late. It might already have you."

WITH *A* full night's sleep under her belt, the things that stalked her in her apartment seemed to be quietened, if not altogether silent.

Taryn did her best to ignore the strange sounds that plagued her, the flashes of light that blasted across the room. She kept her phone close to her hand, ready to dial Matt in an instant should anything happen.

Whatever was there, however, left her alone. It came close enough to let her know it was there, but never close enough to actually bother her. She put on her invisible blinders and worked diligently on her painting, allowing her music to drown out what it could.

A woman had been there with him, she thought. *If not with him when he died then soon after.*

Had it been Ruby? Had she been the one to find him in the motel room? And, if so, then why hadn't she told anyone?

Or had she been there with him all along?

Taryn meant to find answers to her questions, even if they were answers she didn't like.

TWENTY

*S*h*e was on her way to meet with Ruby*, this time at the Loveless Café—a place known for its southern comfort foods. It usually closed early but it was staying open for Ruby.

"Nobody usually bothers me when I'm out," Ruby had told her over the phone, "but this will give us a chance to talk. I've been going there for a long time."

Taryn drove down the road with a lot on her mind. She'd called David but he must have already been on the plane; she'd gone straight to voicemail. She'd left a message instead, thanking him for taking care of her the night before and once again praising his lecture.

Then she'd called Matt and told him about what had happened.

"I don't know that I'm real happy about another man sleeping in your apartment and seeing you in your skivvies," he'd laughed thinly, "but I'm glad he was there to help. You needed that rest and if it couldn't be me there, then I'm glad it was a friend."

"He *is* a friend, Matt," she'd sworn.

233

"Yeah, I know. It's taken me months to get used to that fact, but I know. But still..."

"'Still' what?"

Matt hesitated before speaking. "If something did change, if you started feeling differently... I wouldn't blame you. You'll always be my best friend and I'll always love and support you, no matter who you're with. I truly just want you to be happy."

"I love *you*, Matt," Taryn said sincerely. "I don't want to be with anyone else."

And that was true; she'd always loved Matt. A life without him was unfathomable.

The Loveless Café was a small building on the side of the road. It looked like a little farmhouse from the outside. On the inside, it smelled like biscuits and bacon. A lot of country music singers and other transplants who relocated to Nashville from small, southern towns had flocked there to be reminded of Mama's cooking and home. Taryn's mother, who'd been into whole foods and gluten-free stuff long before they were popular with the hipsters, had not cooked such meals.

But her grandmother had.

As Taryn entered the modest, unpretentious dining establishment she was instantly transported back to her Nana's old farmhouse outside of Franklin—a place that always carried the aroma of fresh flowers, lavender, baby powder, and grease. The whiff of country cooking made her homesick for the woman who had mostly raised her.

Ruby Jane was the only diner but she'd have been easy to spot regardless. Something about her just *glowed*; that was the only word Taryn found close to fitting and even it didn't accurately describe the woman's aura.

Today, Ruby wore skinny jeans, a black turtleneck that was tight enough to be an extra layer of skin, and a bright pink shawl wrapped around her neck. Her long hair with its striking streaks of silver cascaded down her back, long enough for her to nearly sit on it, and it sparkled with tiny diamonds from the sunlight that streaked in through the window and captured it with its rays. She looked like a fairy–ageless and ethereal.

Suddenly, Taryn felt drab and frumpy in her vintage calico dress, saddle shoes, and little brown cardigan. She'd washed and styled her hair but the humidity had frizzed it, leaving it poking out in every direction. She always looked much better in her head than she did in the mirror.

"What a cute dress," Ruby exclaimed as Taryn drew close to the table. "You always look so adorable. I wish I were thirty years younger so that I could wear your clothes!"

It was as if the woman could read her mind, Taryn thought as she sat down.

"Thank you," she replied. "And here I was thinking I always feel so dowdy next to *you*!"

Ruby took a sip of her ice tea and waved her off. "Oh, please. It's not truly me. It's just the fact that I'm old now and can get away with wearing a lot of things that I couldn't when I was younger. Once you reach a certain age people are just impressed that you're not going out in hair curlers."

Taryn wasn't sold. Ruby was probably one of the best dressed women in the business. I was true, however, that she'd never resorted to sporting the western shirts with fringe, long skirts, and cowboy hats that a lot of other women coming up through the music scene of the 1960s and 1970s had been pressed to wear. Instead of a beehive or bouffant, she'd worn her hair long and loose and parted in the middle. Rather than long peasant skirts and shirts with fringe she'd worn black minis and halter tops.

Ruby Jane had always been elegant, always been a *lady*, but had always danced to the beat of her own drum. Now that she was in her sixties and wore African-inspired caftans, southwestern jewelry, and silk saris she was simply carrying on with her own rhythm.

"Do you have more pictures for me?" Ruby asked eagerly, once they'd ordered. "The others you gave me, the copies? Something happened to that SD card. I lost it. I'd be grateful if you could make me another copy."

"No problem," Taryn replied. "I have images, but nothing that contains anything out of the ordinary."

Taryn watched the flicker in the other woman's eyes, a sure sign of disappointment. It was a first for Taryn, the first time anyone had wanted her to seek the paranormal. Of all the times Miss Dixie had picked up on abnormal occurrences—now she *wanted* her to and she couldn't.

"I did take a picture of the canvases I'm working on," Taryn said as she handed Ruby the SD card. "I'm actually finished with the courtyard scene. So you can see it."

Ruby accepted the card and closed her fingers around it.

"We had fun in that courtyard, back in the day," Ruby smiled, glancing down at her silverware. "Park would get out his guitar first and the other would be right behind him. They always waited to see what he was going to do. I was just learning to play back then. I still have trouble tuning. Sometimes I'd have my tambourine. We'd light a fire, pop open a case of beer, and sit around until dawn sometimes, just playing and laughing."

"Did you know he had a problem back then?" Taryn asked, then felt guilty for bringing it up.

Ruby did not look offended, however. "I wasn't naïve. I knew that there were drugs going around. I couldn't have told you what they were or where they got them but I knew they were being used. We even had a road manager who used to hold onto them for the guys and kind of divvy them out to, you know, make sure they didn't get caught with him at the airport or take too much."

"Where was *he* the night Parker died?"

"At home, with his wife. I don't think he's ever forgiven himself for that."

"I imagine things were a lot different back then," Taryn said, thinking of all the stories she'd heard about singers and the drug culture that was more open before the AIDS scare of the 80's took over.

Ruby nodded. "In many ways, yes. I never did any of that stuff. I barely drank. I was too serious, you see. I was so focused on my music. When we first went on tour, however, things we bad. I'd been asked to join the band because they felt like they needed a 'girl singer', as they called it, for harmony. They even stalked me a little bit. Someone told Park about me and he told the others and they kind of dressed incognito and showed up at a bar in the Village I was singing at one night. They wanted to listen to me without me knowing. Of course, I didn't even know who they were. I completely clueless."

Taryn laughed at the idea of the men checking Ruby out, seeing if she had what it took to hang with them.

"But I digress. When we went on that first tour, it was a mess in the beginning. They thought they were so rock and roll, you know? They didn't *need* to rehearse, they didn't *need* a song set, they didn't *need* to get the act together. Winging it was part of the fun. We were actually booed off stage a lot."

Taryn winced. "Yikes."

"I whipped them into shape pretty fast. I finally told them that either we start rehearsing and getting our acts together and doing things my way or I was going back to New York and they could bite me."

"It must have worked!"

"Yes, well." Ruby sighed and took a bite of her omelet. "In hindsight it must have been the drugs making them responsible for a lot of that. I just thought they were carefree, free-spirited souls. It wasn't until much later that I realized just how bad of shape Parker really was."

"He'd cleaned up, though, hadn't he? There at the end?"

"Yes, yes he had. He was doing well. We'd just finished recording that album and were getting ready to go back out on the road. He was clean, probably for the first time since I'd known him. His eyes were clearer, brighter somehow. He was quieter, maybe a little sadder, but he was dealing with things instead of just running away from them..."

Taryn didn't want to press any further. She was surprised Ruby had shared as much with her as she already had.

Both women, lost in their own thoughts, worked steadily on their plates of food. The dining rooms were quiet but, in the back, Taryn could hear the sounds of pots and pans rattling and dishes being washed. The sound of laughter rang out over the country radio station that played softly in the background. Dolly Parton sang about memories that continued to haunt her while Linda Ronstadt and Emmylou Harris harmonized. Taryn thought about the afternoon in the courtyard, when the voice had been right there in her ear.

Before she could bring it up, however, Ruby stopped eating and exhaled slowly. "I do wonder what would've happened if Aker hadn't been with Gloria that night."

Taryn's thoughts were brought to a grinding halt.

"What? Aker?"

"Yes, he was our security guard, kind of our road wrangler when we were out on tour," Ruby explained. "He'd been a cop but I lured him away. He was a big music fan, liked the Byrds, the Stones, some of the folk artists. Dylan. He liked running with the music scene. He toured with us twice and was getting ready to go back out again, but his wife was sick that night and we'd all taken the week off anyway. Kind of scattered in the wind, more or less. We were going to meet back up in Los Angeles in a couple of days."

"I knew you'd known Aker for a long time, but I didn't realize he'd worked with you all," Taryn said slowly.

"Yes, up until Parker died. They were big buddies. Then he returned to the police force. Stayed with them until he was injured on the job and took mandatory retirement. I still take him out on the road with me."

Taryn needed some time to let this digest. But first...

"Ruby, was there a woman there with Parker the night he died? A girlfriend maybe?"

Ruby's face clouded over and she looked down to study her plate. "No," she replied at last. "Parker wasn't seeing anyone at the time. There wasn't anyone there with him. He was alone."

Taryn wanted to know more, to say more, but held herself back. Either Ruby knew something and didn't want to share it with her or Ruby wasn't going to share it at all. Either way, she'd need to tread lightly.

"Ruby... I wasn't sure how to tell you this, but a few days ago when I was working in the courtyard, I was looking at that little shrine of Parker's and," Taryn paused, her face growing hot.

"Yes?" Ruby eagerly leaned forward, her eyes glistening.

"A voice quoted a line from an old Irish prayer. And it was very, very close. Like, right on top of me. I could feel the breath on my skin." Taryn felt goosebumps on her arms just thinking about it. "I wasn't scared. In fact, it was kind of nice."

Ruby leaned back in her seat and exhaled loudly. "People have told me over the years that he's still there, that he can't leave. I don't understand that. Parker would never be trapped anywhere. He never liked staying in one spot. He was always moving around, always on the go. But I've wondered why, after all these years, he's never once come to me. No matter how much I've prayed and prayed, and cried for him to come see me and show me he's okay."

"Maybe he *can't*," Taryn whispered, looking around the room to ensure nobody could hear them. They were still alone.

"Do you think it was him, Taryn? Do you think it was Parker?"

She wanted so badly to tell her yes, to tell her that her partner's spirit was still on the grounds of that awful place, but she couldn't be certain. And she wasn't going to lie. "I don't know," Taryn replied honestly. "I wish I did. But if it is him, what do you think he meant by 'remember'?"

Ruby shook her head. "I wish I knew that. But I don't. Can you find out for me? Can you help me? I've spent the past forty-six years trying to make peace with this. I'm afraid I never will, not until I can be sure he's at peace."

"I'll try," Taryn promised her. "I'll do my best."

Aker, she thought. *Aker had spent time at that motel, had been friends with Parker.*

It wasn't like he had to share anything with her, but she found it strange that, during their meal, he hadn't mentioned knowing Parker at all. Very strange.

"SO *WHAT* do you need from *me*?" Matt asked.

"Research," Taryn answered. "I want you to read anything you can about Parker Brown's early life and then jump to the events on the night he died. I want to try to understand the psychology behind the drug use and figure out if anything happened that night that might have been missed."

"You think it wasn't an overdose?" Matt asked. "From what you've told me, it sure sounds like it was."

"If that's him hanging around the motel, then there's a reason," Taryn said. "I want to know what that reason is."

"Could just be that it was an accidental overdose, he didn't mean to die, and he's not ready to leave. That he thinks his life is still going on," Matt reasoned.

"Could be, could be. And it could be something else. Let's cover our bases."

"Do you really think that Parker's disgruntled spirit is making you manic, though? And messing with you by banging the door shut, knocking things over, and stuff? That doesn't sound like a ghost that wants something from you. Not anything good, anyway."

"I don't know," Taryn replied. "I guess if he's upset that he can't move on, and mad that's dead to begin with, then he could have some rage built up in him. Death does strange thing to the living–just think of what it might be doing to the dead."

"Now there's a book," Matt mused thoughtfully. "*The Five Stages of Grief for the Dead: How to Enjoy Your Afterlife without Bugging the Living.*"

"I'd start carrying copies around with me."

TWENTY-ONE

With the courtyard completed, Taryn meant to get started on the lobby next.

Her last experience with Room #5 had been a little too exciting for her taste. She was trying to learn to distance herself emotionally from some of the things that happened to her but, the truth was, she couldn't. She took everything personally. The fear she'd initially experienced of the paranormal inviting itself into her life wasn't quite as consuming as it has been in the beginning but she was still only human; she still got frightened, still had trouble sleeping after something unsettled her, and looked over her shoulder a lot to ensure nothing was behind her.

Even more than the fear was the sensitivity she felt to the emotions the experiences brought about. She'd yet to meet a jolly, happy spirit. Just like the living, they dragged their baggage with them and she was more or less their luggage handler on the connecting flight.

Sometimes the sadness, fear, and anger became too much for her. After Jekyll Island she'd learned to take breaks, cool herself down a little.

Distance herself.

She'd planned on doing that with Room #5.

It wasn't quite working.

Instead, it just pulled out the big guns.

IT *TOOK* a lot of creative energy, and more than a few hours researching hotels constructed in the same time period, to recreate the lobby. Considering the sorry shape it was now in, even Taryn was having trouble seeing past the ruin to what it must have once looked like.

It couldn't have always been that bad. Right?

She'd once worked on a lodge out west for six weeks. It was once of those places built for a state park. Built back when families used to load everyone up in the car and take them on grand tours of the Grand Canyon and Death Valley, stopping at every state line to file the tired kids out one by one and position them in front of the "welcome" sign to pose for the sake of posterity. Built before roadside motor lodges and pancakes were replaced by Disney cruises and all-you-can-eat buffets.

The lodge in question was run down and neglected. Though not without hope, it was a far cry from the spit and polish high rises of nearby Las Vegas. Much different than those overwhelming monstrosities that took up ten acres of land and had you worn out from their colorful, busy carpets and two-mile hike to the exit before you even made it out to the blistering heat rising from the pavement of the Strip.

She'd been hired to paint the lobby. At one time the lobby had sported an Art Deco style, somewhat out of place in the desert's simple coarseness but architecturally pleasing just the same. Bits of that Art Deco still existed in a few of the light fixtures that managed to hide from the multiple renovations throughout the years, but, for the most part, by the time Taryn got to it, the lobby was a mishmash of clashing colors, styles, and textures. It looked like ten contestants with over-inflated egos from "Design Star" had all drawn ten different time periods out of a box and were instructed to use nothing but items found in a landfill.

And... go!

"The heat here gets to a lot of people," the hotel's general manager had warned her. "Between it and the glare of the sun, some people find they have a lot of trouble this time of year."

It was true she'd gone through more than her fair share of Excedrin Migraine that summer, but the temperature and sunlight had nothing to do with it. She still couldn't hear the phrase "mid-century modern" without being reminded of the awful uncomfortable, stained, (once) white chairs that flanked the beautiful hand-carved fireplace (painted magenta during what *had* to have been someone's acid trip in the 1960s).

Just about every unique, original feature in that lobby had been destroyed, tainted, ruined, or removed. It had been incredibly difficult for her to see past the heinous interior design and sad neglect the lack of funds had caused. It was deteriorating at a rapid pace.

Still, the old girl had some spunk left in her and eventually, once Taryn got to know her and became familiar with her bones through the eyes of her own imagination and Miss Dixie, she'd been able to work with what she had. The result had been a glorious window into the past, a stunning recreation of a lobby that spoke not just of a style popularized in a decade known for fun and opulence, but of a more innocent time when families could still be charmed by the unpretentious entertainment provided by the simplicity of nature. When board games together in the lobby, not fast Wi-Fi, had brought everyone together in the evenings.

She could *not* see past the ugliness of Black Raven Inn's lobby.

"It's not you, it's me," she told the drab, dreary little place.

She didn't think that anything could make it look better—nothing short of a complete overhaul and massive renovation.

The space was too small, the layout too awkward (the weird "L" shape made it cramped for the guests checking it and gave the staff little room in which to maneuver), and the lack of adequate windows made it too dark.

"I'm just going to recreate it from scratch," she declared, scrapping her original idea of using the old photos of the motel for inspiration. "We'll call it more of an 'inspired by' painting than a 'recreation.'"

She didn't think Ruby would mind.

With new resolution, she set off to start faintly sketching her painting with confidence. She'd make it the best darn lobby that the Black Raven Inn had ever seen.

Not that it would take much.

She'd barely drawn the outline of the perimeter, however, when the low, mournful singing began permeating the room. It drifted through the walls, soft and low at first, a man's sweet, warbling tenor. Taryn hesitated with her charcoal held aloft, barely breathing. She hardly dared to breathe.

The singing voice was not pitch perfect; it was tentative and reedy, almost thin in some places. She listened as it strained to hit the higher notes and then fell dipped back down, catching itself in its hesitation. It probably would not have been played on today's radio, at least not before an over-zealous producer got ahold of it with some auto pitch and made the artist suffer through endless takes.

Still, there was something soothing and beautiful about its frailty. Under the imperfections was a heavy emotional undercurrent that enraptured Taryn and threatened to lift her off the ground and carry her away. The sadness engulfed her, playing to her sensitivities, until she wanted to cry. He was singing nonsense, something about dancing and maybe even a bird or a likewise peculiar entity but she didn't care. The beauty of the music was immeasurable.

Taryn knew it was Parker Brown. She'd listened to the three albums he'd made with the band and would have known his voice anywhere. This was not a recording, however. This was the real Parker, just him and his guitar. He was there in the room with her, singing to her, and reaching down into her heart—pulling something up from her by the strings.

For a moment Taryn closed her eyes and let herself fall. She imagined being Ruby Jane, young and falling in love with the man who created such beautiful music.

She envisioned her sitting outside with the others, or alone in a cheap motel room on the road, being serenaded by him in the middle of the night while everyone else in the world was asleep. Sitting cross-legged on the a sagging bed, motel-room refrigerator humming beside her, a bedsheet pulled up to her neck to cover her otherwise exposed chest, watching his fingers (the same fingers that had just played over her skin) strum the strings with tenderness. Knowing that while the rest of the world thought he was *theirs*, at that one moment he was *hers*, and nobody else's. What kind of power that much have been, what kind of heat.

Taryn's heart ached for the sorrow of the melody and heartbreak in the voice. She thought of her own losses, of the hole in her heart that had mended several times but continued to grow even under the scar tissue.

She began to weaken, thinking of Parker and the terrible loss Ruby must have felt, of the undeniable tragedy and senselessness his death had been.

Taryn shook her head and muttered, "*Damn* it, Parker, just a little bit more. Just a little bit longer. If you just could have made it..."

"Why did he die?" she'd asked her grandmother when she was nine, after learning a family friend had committed suicide. "Why did he use that gun?"

"Because," her grandmother had answered unhappily, running a brush with care through Taryn's still silky little-girl hair. They were on their way to the funeral.

"Because *why*?"

"Because he was just too sad and wanted to feel better."

Just too sad...

The singing continued and Taryn felt the charcoal tenderly removed from her fingers and descend to the floor, where the long, thin stick broke in two. She reached down and picked half of it up just as the canvas in front of her was gently lifted and released to the ground at her feet. The wooden easel fell over in one fluid movement, the crash softened by the muddy shag carpet.

He was close to her now, whispering into her ear. She could feel him as much as she could hear him. His lips were practically on her skin, seductive and inviting. If she reached back with her hands just a little, she thought she might be able to touch him, but she didn't try. To make something solid of it would be to spoil it. She wasn't ready for that; curiosity beset her.

And then she was paralyzed with fear, a prisoner within her own body. To have the desire to walk, run, and cry out but yet feel as though the body couldn't remember how to do those things...*that* was almost the most terrifying thing of all.

For Taryn, the seduction, the *gentleness*, was just as horrific as the anger and temper–perhaps even more so. The anger was madness; it was hostility. The fury and rage were, together, a volcano of heat and uninhabited pressure–the eruption of bottled-up emotions, pent-up frustration, which could not be contained.

The anger was not human, it was something wild and animalistic that could only be found in untamed, uncontrollable nature.

This, though...*this* was controlled. This was *deliberate*.

It knew what it was doing and more disturbingly, did it for a *reason*. It had a purpose and a method.

Even more painful, Taryn thought as the icy fear that chilled her feet and froze her hands fought with the burning heat that flooded through her chest and sent her head spinning, *even worse was that it knew what would get to her*. He'd watched her, gotten inside her mind (and worse, her heart) and knew what she was all about.

"No," she whispered, her voice hoarse and raspy with dread.

He had her number.

When the fury and irrepressible violence had worked only to frighten her but not sway her, when the manic obsession and mental anguish of working without stopping and sleeping had not deterred her from her path, it turned to the one thing she couldn't fight–desolation. Throw sadness at her and she weakened. Taryn's kryptonite was grief, both her own and that of those around her. It pulled her in and drowned her every time.

The singing stopped and Taryn could breathe easier. She was shaking, but she could breathe. She wanted to call Matt. Hell, she wanted to call *David*, but she couldn't.

This would follow her. Whatever Parker wanted from her, he wouldn't give up until he had it. She'd already seen that.

Shaky, and still clutching the stick of charcoal, Taryn let herself out of the lobby, using the back door that led to the courtyard. Following breadcrumbs dropped by an unseen hand, she strode down the overgrown sidewalk, her sneakers flattening the thorny weeds that grabbed at her legs and tried to attach themselves to her legs.

Room #5 was soon before her, a gingerbread house made entirely of candy, the icing and gumdrops the faint guitar chords that resounded through the rickety door.

She extended the broken piece of charcoal to the door knob, Gretel with the chicken bone fooling the blind old witch.

Sparks threatened to fly from the metal but, without the contact of her skin, fizzled out.

It was all a façade, a trick to get her in the oven. There was no melancholy singer with a beautiful soul waiting for her to rescue him. There couldn't be a deeper connection that drew her to him, something beyond either one of them.

There was only heat and fire, intent on burning her until it got what it needed.

Taryn entered the room.

TWENTY—TWO

Taryn *was roasting in the sweltering heat.* She was so hot she'd removed her sweater, kicked off her shoes, and tied her Rodney Crowell T-shirt in a knot by her bellybutton–something she hadn't done since high school.

She might have had a fever. They were having a weird hot spell, with temperatures soaring into the mid-eighties, but it still didn't explain the sauna that Room #5 had become. It usually ran at least ten degrees colder inside than it did out there where Aker was waiting for her.

Her phone beeped and Taryn glanced down at it. It was Matt. "P.B. became paranoid in the last few weeks of his life. Friends said he thought the FBI was after him."

Taryn sent a quick reply then returned to the canvas. It wasn't unusual for famous people to start feeling paranoia. The paparazzi, as it was now, wouldn't have been the same for Parker but that didn't mean people weren't still watching him, observing him. Not only had he been famous himself, but he'd run in circles with even bigger celebrities and the press had tailed them.

Taryn reached down and took a big swig of water from a water bottle she'd started carrying around. She'd been locking herself in the room for a week now, working on the painting. In that time she'd found herself craving liquids, a thirst so deep she could never really get enough. At first the thirst had only hit her while she was in the room. After the first two days, however, it had followed her home. She was spending too much money on Coke and Mountain Dew, sometimes going through an entire twelve pack by supper. She'd turned to juice, but upon discovering that she could tilt it up and down the whole half gallon in less than an hour she'd moved on to water.

She wasn't hungry, she was barely eating at all, but she couldn't get enough to drink. Her insides felt like a desert.

"Ahhhh," she sighed with relief, before taking another swig. The water was still ice cold. She wondered how it was able to keep its coolness surrounded by such heat.

The mirror on the wall flickered, catching her eye. Taryn turned and studied it. Things like that had been happening all day. At first she thought it was the bulbs in her spotlights going out but she never saw them waver. It was definitely something in the mirror.

Taryn slowly walked towards the glass and placed her hand on the surface. Her pale reflection gazed back at her. She thought she'd lost weight. Her eyes looked big and sunken into her face, her lips dry and thin. She was tired because she hadn't been sleeping well.

The glass under her hand burned from the heat. It occurred to her that, once again, she was looking into an object that had acted as guard and reflection for that room for decades. How much had it seen? How much did it know? Were the actions of the past still trapped in it somehow, forever replaying their sequence over and over again?

"How much do you know?" she asked it.

Something in the glass shimmered, as if in reply.

When Taryn returned to her painting she bent over again and grabbed the water bottle. Sweat rolled down her face and dripped from her hair.

She'd have to wear something more lightweight tomorrow.

"DID *RUBY* say anything about Parker being a hoarder?" Matt asked.

Taryn paused and looked up from Miss Dixie. She was busy cleaning her lens while she had her nightly chat. "A hoarder? No, nothing like that."

"I found a kind of obscure interview from a few years ago," he told her, "done with one of the other guys. It was about his new album and in the middle he threw in something about Parker's house in California being 'unhealthy' and a 'mess.' There's a picture of a bathroom here, with the sink and tub kind of covered with shampoo bottles, bath gel, all kinds of stuff. You can't see any surface."

"That's weird," Taryn replied. "I always thought of Parker as nomadic. I wouldn't have thought he was someone who didn't get rid of things."

"Well, maybe there at the end that's just what started happening," Matt mused. "He could've been sick in a lot of ways."

Back in her own apartment, she was finally able to cool off. In fact, she was even a little chilly. Going from hot to cool was going to make her sick, she just knew it. She seriously needed to stock up on some vitamins and fresh fruit and vegetables. Stuff like bananas and apples and kale. Spinach. Fruit rollups and spinach and artichoke flavored chips weren't going to count. Unfortunately.

"Hey, I'm not feeling too well," Taryn began.

"EDS stuff?"

"Nah, I think I'm coming down with a cold or something like that. It's this weather. But I was wondering if you knew some foods or supplements I could add to my diet to boost my immune system. Maybe some recipes? Something that's going to go easy on my tummy," Taryn added, "since it's a little fragile at the moment."

"You still throwing up?" Matt asked in concern.

"Yeah, but not as often," Taryn lied. Truthfully, she was still vomiting at least once a day. Sometimes more.

"I've got some recipes I can send you," Matt said. "Some easy things I think you can make."

"Are you making fun of me?" Taryn demanded, only half joking. While it was true that Matt loved cooking, and considered himself an experienced and talented chef, she could actually cook as well–and cook *well*. Matt forgot that. A lot.

"No, no, no," he sang. "I just thought that if you were feeling poorly you'd probably rather have something that didn't take a lot of time and effort to prepare."

"Yeah, well..." She couldn't exactly argue with logic like that.

"Are you chilled?"

"No, actually feeling hot," Taryn replied.

"Fever?"

"I thought I did but I checked it as I've been talking to you and it's fine. A little on the low side at 96, but that's my normal."

"Cough? Stuffy nose? Aches and pains?" he pressed.

"Yes and no, Dr. Matt," she laughed. "Some drainage, a bit of a cough, and I have no idea if there are any new aches and pains or not."

"Good point. It's probably just a cold; your system could be going haywire from the weather changing like it is."

"At least the room I'm working in is warm. It was so cold in the beginning. I guess maybe the heat finally kicked in or something because now I can hardly stand it. It's like being in a sauna. And it makes me so thirsty."

"At least it's a dry heat," Matt said.

Taryn snorted. "'Dry heat?' Have you ever stuck your head in an oven? That's dry heat too. Lack of humidity of not, it's still *hot*."

Matt chuckled and began telling her about his day and his students. Before he hung up he returned the conversation to Parker. "The hoarding reference is the only thing I've come across so far that's new—something that hasn't been written about over and over again already. All most people want to write about is his death in that hotel room."

Matt said this last part in distaste. He wasn't big on public displays of attention or notoriety. Although he knew that what went on with Taryn wasn't her fault, and that she didn't invite media attention in when they picked up her stories, he had trouble sometimes receiving the attention by proxy. The idea of someone continuously writing about his sudden, tragic death for decades to come probably filled him with trepidation—and *not* the kind Taryn got from her adventures with the undead.

"I appreciate your help, dude," Taryn said as a reply. "I've said it before and I'll say it again...you kind of missed your calling as a private investigator."

"There's one more thing, though," Matt began with a hint of hesitancy.

"What's up, buttercup?"

"Aker. This guy who's acting as your security detail?"

"Yeah, I know who Aker is..."

"How much do you know about him?"

"Little to nothing," Taryn admitted. "He's apparently been around for a long time, though. He worked for Ruby and Parker back in the day. I think he might feel guilty that he wasn't there when Parker overdosed."

"Well, apparently some people thought he was there," Matt said slowly. "Years later his wife, or ex-wife now I guess, came forward and said that he wasn't home with her that night. She'd lied to give him an alibi."

Taryn felt unease settle in around her collar as she thought of Aker in his dark sunglasses and tight muscles, bald head reflecting the sunlight, book in hand. They were starting to feel a little more comfortable around each other but had not developed a friendship of any kind. He tolerated her, more or less.

"Do you think he was there at the hotel with Parker when he overdosed?" she asked.

"I hope not," Matt replied. "If he was, then why didn't he call the police?"

Why, indeed?

TWENTY-THREE

Lenny Parsons opened Ruby's door, barefoot and disheveled. It was 6:00 pm and the sky was graying with the impending darkness, but he looked like he'd just woken up.

"Hey, Karen right?" he asked, stepping aside to let Taryn walk through the door.

"It's Taryn, actually," she replied as she walked into the dimly lit foyer. She was torn between feeling prideful enough to correct him and flattered that he was at least close.

"Sorry, Taryn," he said absently.

Taryn followed him through the house to the back, where sliding doors welcomed them to a beautifully landscaped patio. Ruby sat on the flagstones, two rambunctious puppies rolling around in her lap and licking her face. Her black yoga pants were covered in dog hair, her red cotton T-shirt stained, and her hands damp from dog slobber. She looked positively happy, though, as she fussed the two yapping Pomeranians and occasionally reached up to brush her tangled hair from her face.

"Sorry Taryn," she apologized. "I'm fostering these little guys and they're pretty excited to be here."

"I can see that," Taryn smiled. "They're pretty cute."

Taryn sat down on the ground with her, a few feet away. With a new audience, the puppies bounded with glee towards her, falling over each other as they raced to see who would reach her first. She soon found herself under a blanket of dogs, coarse little tongues leaving a trail of kisses over her neck and cheeks.

"They're, uh, excited," Taryn laughed as she grabbed one under one arm and one under the other and attempted to quiet them. They looked from Taryn to Ruby in adoration, as though they couldn't believe their good fortune.

"I foster them when I can, when I know I'm not going to be on the road for awhile," Ruby explained. "I like having them around. Lenny's not much of a fan though, are you?"

Lenny plopped down in an outdoor chair and cracked open a bottle of Belgium beer. He knocked back half the bottle in one swill then belched under his breath. "Nope."

Ruby rolled her eyes. "He's not into puppies or babies," she confided to Taryn.

"Don't tell the fans," he grinned. "It will hurt my image."

Taryn remembered a popular poster, sold in the electronic sections of some big-box stores, of Lenny sitting under a tree with a litter of puppies frolicking at his feet. She could only imagine the number of women that pestered him into posing with their toddlers and infants at autograph sessions.

She wondered what other uncomfortable positions entertainers put themselves in for the sake of marketing.

"So how's that old dump treating you?" Lenny asked. "It's been years since I was inside that old thing."

"Well, it's old," Taryn replied. "And not in very good shape."

She didn't want to complain about its condition too much, at least not in front of Ruby who was both her employer and had a sentimental attachment to it. It felt rude.

Lenny snorted. "Should tear it down. Don't know what the hell Stretch here is doing with it. She obviously needs a hobby."

Taryn glanced over at Ruby, who listened but wasn't reacting. Ruby was now propped back on her hands, her long legs stretched out in front of her. Taryn was mildly surprised that Ruby had not shared her true intentions with Lenny but had with her. Then again, she was learning that some people had trouble talking about the paranormal with others, even those they'd known most of their lives. It wasn't easy admitting that you believe in ghosts, much less that you were looking for them, when you weren't sure if the person you were talking to was going to ridicule or support you.

"I've been working on the room," she offered to Ruby. "I just wanted to stop by and give you an update. I had to take a few days off for my health but I've been making them up and should still make the deadline."

Ruby smiled sweetly and waved Taryn's concerns away. "It's fine. You have you have to take care of *you*."

"I've enjoyed looking at some of the pictures and posters and things people have left in his room," Taryn said. She'd actually come there to talk to Ruby about what was going on, but no longer felt comfortable doing so with Lenny's presence.

"People always did like going there and saying their goodbyes," Ruby agreed. "Used to be that they'd stock the room with real memorabilia, like a toothbrush he left hind or a letter he'd sent to the motel and stuff, but then people just started stealing them. A little morbid if you ask me."

"Poor old Parker," Lenny grunted. "People never will let him go. The guy's dead. Everyone just needs to move on."

Ruby stiffened and Taryn instantly felt sorry for her. The implication was clear; Ruby was the one who needed to "move on." Taryn had heard it all before after Andrew died...

At least he's in a better place...

God needed another angel...

Now he'll always be able to watch over you from Heaven...

You need to get out more and find someone new...

He'd want you to be happy...

At least he didn't suffer...

Only the good die young...

When are you going to get over it...

You need to move on...

The most well-meaning and unhelpful advice came from those who had never lost a partner or anyone real close. At first the platitudes, clichés that made the people who said them feel better for trying to help but offered no real comfort to her, frustrated her. Then they made her angry.

Why was everyone so intent that she "move on"? What did that even mean? Why did it matter to them? It was funny how that advice always came from people she rarely saw—people who almost never came around her. It's not like she was bugging them with talks of Andrew or running them into the ground with her grief and sadness and yet, there they were, pressing her to "let him go."

It made her mad enough to want to hold on even more.

"Well, I just stopped in to give you an update," Taryn said, rising to her feet. She was just ornery enough that the idea of humming Lenny's big hit "Never Let You Go" ran through her mind but, in the end, she decided that might be a bit much. "It's been a long day and I need to get home."

"I'll walk you out," Ruby said, also standing. She brushed her hands along the back of her yoga pants, sending dog hair flying. Lenny flinched and wrinkled his nose.

The puppies ran around in circles, worried and confused. Their ladies were leaving. Taryn watched with interest as they avoided Lenny completely. It was true that dogs could sense who didn't want them or like them. Who might be mean to them.

"Bye," Taryn waved to Lenny over her shoulder. "It was nice to see you again."

He muttered something similar and then took another swig from his bottle, emptying it.

"I wanted to talk to you about some things going on at the motel," Taryn explained as they slowly made their way through the house. "I didn't feel real comfortable doing it with your friend here."

Ruby rolled her eyes and patted Taryn on the arm. "Yes, Lenny's never been a fan of those kinds of things. He's not much of a believer in anything he can't see to shoot."

"Was he a friend to Parker?" Taryn asked.

"Good friends. They were buddies. Lenny took his death hard. He was never quite the same after, although he did quit the hard stuff. Of course, the booze was something else," Ruby laughed. "I think he's more beer than blood at this point."

"I wanted to ask you about Aker," Taryn said as they neared the front door. "Were he and Parker friends?"

"Not friends so much as a professional relationship," Ruby replied. "Aker took his job very seriously."

"Yeah, he does that now, too."

"I don't think he was much of a fan. Aker never agreed with the drug usage that all the guys did. He took care of them, but there was a bit of judgment there. Of course, the fact that Parker courted Aker's ex-wife didn't win him any favors."

Taryn paused. "Parker had a thing with Aker's ex-wife?"

"Well, they weren't married at the time. Aker was married to Gloria by then. You know how men are, though,"

Ruby laughed. "Territorial, just like we are. I thought, when Aker found out, that it would be the end of him and his employment with us. They seemed to work it out, though. Parker didn't mean anything serious by it. He just got lonely. I think it bothered him that Aker took it personally. He never wanted to hurt anyone."

Ruby looked down then and narrowed her eyes, her face hardening.

Except you, Taryn thought. *He hurt* you.

"One more thing. Was Parker a, for lack of better word, hoarder there at the end?"

"Well, not like those people you see on TV—the ones with all the plastic containers of urine and four feet of garbage in all the rooms," Ruby explained. "But he did have some issues. He was very ill there at the end, sicker than any of us knew. I wish I had known. I wish I'd known as much as I thought I did."

TARYN *LOOKED* at the computer screen again and sadly shook her head. Who would be so hateful? Who could possibly hate her *that* much?

A lot of her clients found her through an online freelancing site for artists. She had a portfolio there and there was even an escrow system available to make payment easier for both parties involved. Former clients could leave reviews, similar to what visitors could find on sites like Yelp and Tripadvisor.

Up until now, Taryn's reviews had been stellar, her feedback excellent.

Not anymore.

"A total hack job," she read aloud to Matt, her voice shaking. "This so-called 'artist' wasn't much better than an elementary school kid with a box of watercolors. I could've done better work with crayons. We hired her to paint a building that meant a lot to us and it became obvious that we were overpaying her from the very beginning. No technique, cookie cutter results, and no depth or soul to her work. Avoid at all costs."

Unable to hold it together any longer, Taryn put her head down and burst into tears. Matt was quiet on the other end of the line, allowing her to cry and get it all out.

"I'm sorry," he said at last. "I don't think it's real, though. It sounds like someone just trying to be mean."

"Yeah well," she sniffed, "they succeeded."

"Your clients love you," he insisted. "You've never worked with anyone who wasn't happy with your work. This isn't real."

"It doesn't matter, Matt. Potential clients will see this and think it is."

"You want to call Rob, have him do a little hacking and figure it out? He might be able to trace it…"

Rob was their mutual friend. He lived in Lexington, Kentucky where he ran a store called New Age Gifts and More. The "and more" consisted of electronics he bought cheap, fixed up, and sold for profit. On one side of his store you could find crystal balls, incense, and brightly colored candles. On the other it was DVD players, flat-screens, and refurbished iPads.

"Yeah, can you do that?" she asked. "I'd really like to know who did it. Someone I've obviously pissed off."

Now that she'd had a bit of a cry, she was shaking mad. How dare someone try to sabotage her reputation like that? It was a bully, and Taryn didn't tolerate bullies.

"Whoever did it can suck my toe," she hissed.

"Well, they can suck mine too. And my kneecap and heel," Matt threw in for good measure.

Taryn offered a watery smile over the line but she was reeling from the offensive review. What the hell was *wrong* with people anyway?

THE *WOMAN* with the peroxide blonde hair leaned back beside him, her black silk panties and bra shiny in the soft glow of the lamplight. Her hair was mussed, her lipstick smudged, and she puffed heartily at a cigarette.

The man beside her was stretched out on the bed, the lower half of his body covered by the sheets. He had his hands crossed under his head as he appeared to stare at the ceiling fan above.

The look on her face was a smug one, full of pride at what she'd just done. The look on his face was of contempt, as though slightly ashamed of the act.

A mini skirt was draped over the arm of the chair. Red high heels had been kicked off by the door. A shirt was hanging from the doorknob leading into the bathroom. Whatever had occurred there in the room, And Taryn didn't have to read too much into it to know the answer, had happened quickly. There had been a lot of passion in the act, but now that it was over with there didn't seem to be much love.

Taryn couldn't tear her eyes away from the picture on her LCD screen, even though she was clearly peeking in on an intimate act.

"Did you really have to share this one with me, Miss Dixie?"

The LCD screen went black and then abruptly turned back on again, as though Miss Dixie was giving her a slight wink.

"Very funny," she said drily.

The picture was of Parker, of course, but she didn't know who the woman was. She'd never seen her before.

Taryn looked back up and studied the room in front of her again. It was odd to think that she was standing in the very place where the woman's high heels had been kicked off, that her own shoes now took that spot.

"Oh Parker," she whispered to the room. "What did you do to Ruby? Why did you have to break her heart?"

The silent room lit up like a Christmas tree, both lamps and the overhead light going on at full blast. Taryn suddenly found herself in a spotlight, on display. The ceiling fan began spinning around and around in circles, so fast that the arms were a black blur against the white ceiling. The bathroom door slammed to with a bang; the chair next to her fell over with a crash.

"Parker!" Taryn cried over the din, covering her ears with her hands. "Stop it, Parker! Stop it!"

The room was quiet again, silenced as though someone had pulled the plug on the noise.

The last of the lights faded and went off, leaving Taryn standing there in the dark, alone.

TWENTY-FOUR

The heat was getting to Taryn again. Her tummy gurgled, a sound that threatened to bring up the meager contents she'd ingested for breakfast. She rubbed at it with her free hand, subconsciously attempting to soothe it through touch.

The walls in the room appeared to ripple through the waves of heat, making her feel like she was on a ship being tossed on the waves in a squall, as she suddenly struggled to stand. She collapsed back in the chair behind her as the objects in the room began to swim in her unfocused gaze, making her dizzy.

The only artwork in the motel room that didn't have anything to do with Parker Brown was a print of a horse grazing in the middle of a field. The field, with its iridescent green grass enclosed by a stone fence, reminded her of something she'd seen in Central Kentucky. The horse was saddled and ready for a ride. It looked straight at Taryn with its mouth full, its soulful eyes penetrating through her layers of clothing until she felt it could see right down to her skin.

Taryn could've sworn that only the day before that horse had been emerging from the barn, undressed, and with a foal at its side.

She shook her head and closed her eyes.

Had that painting even been there on her first day? She could no longer remember.

A row of water bottles lined the floor at her feet. She was no longer stopping for lunch breaks; she'd enter the motel room early in the morning, sometimes as early as 7:00 am, and wouldn't leave until it got dark—not emerging until her hands were cramped and the sun was setting.

Aker was looking concerned but hadn't said anything to her. She figured that as long as he saw that she was alive he was content that he could continue collecting his paycheck.

The guitar music that sometimes played started up now, a folksy melody that reminded her of some of the Rolling Stones' acoustic work. Like always, it came from everywhere and nowhere at the same time.

The music no longer frightened Taryn. She was even starting to enjoy it.

When the room stopped swimming, Taryn opened the fourth water bottle and consumed the contents in less than a minute. She'd been cooking the meals Matt emailed her but couldn't eat more than a few bites at a time. Still, they were providing the nutrients she needed to stay alive.

Her small frame was growing smaller by the day, however. Her stomach was now not just flat but concave; her legs were starting to look like sticks.

Worst of all, she was losing her butt. She'd always been kind of proud of her behind. It was pert and plump and stuck out at a pleasing angle.

Now it was getting as flat as a pancake.

The bed looked cleaner today. In fact, the whole room appeared cleaner. Gone were the animal excrement, stale scent of garbage and decay, and even the buildup of dust and dirt. She wasn't sure when that had happened.

At some point that afternoon the electricity had decided to work as well. Both lamps in the motel's room had flickered on, casting an eerie glow over the furniture and walls. The shadows danced before her now, growing tall on the walls and casting themselves across the ceiling before quickly shrinking and plummeting to the floor again.

With each movement, the shadows stretched just a little further across the ceiling, growing closer to closer to where she sat with her easel. Soon, they'd be above her. Taryn shrank from them, wary of their spindly hands that reached outward in every direction, seeking something they never seemed to find. They got worse when she paused in her painting.

A crash from the bathroom and the sound of running water has Taryn getting to her feet and following the noise. The shower curtain rod had fallen, leaving the mildewed fabric in a dirty heap on the floor. She hated that small, cramped room. There was barely enough space to breathe in there. When she had to go to the bathroom she took a break and told Aker, who kept an eye on things while she jumped in her car and made way for the coffee shop a few blocks over.

Aker apparently never had to pee. For some reason, this was not an issue for him.

When Taryn re-entered the bedroom, the first thing she noticed was that the painting of the horse was gone. In its place was a concert poster, advertising a show with Parker's band opening for The Byrds. The lamps were out again, leaving the room darker but less menacing without the disturbing shadows. The mouse droppings and smell of urine had returned but the room was still blazing hot.

Miss Dixie looked at her from the nightstand. Taryn thought she might have winked.

"What have you done?" she asked her camera, shaking her head. "Was this you?"

When she picked her up, Taryn noticed right away that the camera was on. Her battery was nearly depleted. "Have you been on this whole time?"

Not only had she been on, but she'd taken pictures as well. There were at least half a dozen shots on the SD card that she hadn't taken. Taryn stood in the middle of the room, temporarily forgetting the blistering heat, and flicked through the images.

The room in the picture didn't look that much different than what it had looked like just a few minutes before–the same mirror hung on the wall, the same generic equine painting was by the closet, the same nightstands with their lights on flanked the bed...

"What am I looking at, old girl," Taryn said. "I'm having a hard time getting the picture here."

Getting the picture...

It was then Taryn realized that for most of the afternoon, as Miss Dixie had been "on" and taking her random shots of the room, she'd turned on the past again. Only, this time, Taryn had been *in* her camera. The room had looked different then because she'd been in the frame.

Taryn had traveled back in time through her lens.

"Well. That's different."

It didn't explain the walls, or the horse moving in the painting, or a number of other things that were threatening to drive Taryn insane.

"I'm going to have to start carrying a penny around with me I guess," she said shakily. "Something to bring me back to the present."

Taryn walked around the room, looking at the same things she'd been staring at for the past week.

She owed Parker nothing. She owed this motel nothing.

Her head was pounding, her stomach gurgled in hunger she couldn't satisfy, her body was on fire, and the very thing that seemed to want her help was threatening to drive her insane.

And she couldn't, for the life of her, walk away.

"REALLY? *FIFTY*-FIVE people? Are you sure that's right?"

"Taryn, I swear to God I am not exaggerating," David swore. "And that's not even counting the ones who had heart attacks, strokes, stuff like that. These are just the murders, the overdoses, the random accidents..."

"So you're telling me that over the past, I don't know, seventy years the Black Raven Inn has had more than fifty deaths?"

"Yep."

"Dang."

Taryn half-heartedly pushed a buggy down the grocery store aisle, searching for food that would stretch her money the farthest. Pre-packaged food was not created for single people. How could she possibly eat a box of macaroni and cheese by herself when it was meant to feed four? Why were the only single versions of food frozen or microwavable?

"Now, they weren't all in that same room," David said.

Taryn stopped in front of a row of soup cans and studied them. She could remember back when chicken noodle and tomato were the main options. Now there was half an aisle dedicated to them. It was all overwhelming.

"Well, that's something at least."

She was surprised at how chilly the grocery store was, how cool it was outside. It had been a shock to her system to step outside the sweltering hotel room. She'd looked silly in her rolled-up tank top and flip flops, when Aker was wearing a down jacket and gloves. He'd looked at her strangely but hadn't said anything.

"Anyway, I just wanted to let you know," David said. "When I got back to Georgia I decided to do some research on it myself."

"Thanks, I appreciate it. Did you happen to find anything else out?"

"Just that lots of bad things seem to happen there. But I guess that's not surprising considering the type of place it became, and the people it drew."

"Anything about Parker?"

David signed. "Only that he was a talented musician who died before his time and suffered from a big drug problem. Same old story, unfortunately."

"Yeah," Taryn said sadly, "same old story."

TWENTY-FIVE

Taryn tried to reconcile the happy, sweet looking boy in the pictures with the anger and fury that ran rampant in the motel room.

She couldn't.

Parker Brown's boyish face looked out from the old photographs with the hopefulness of youth, blissfully ignorant of the fact that he'd be dead in just a few short years. As Taryn scrolled through the photos of him she'd unearthed on the internet she couldn't help but think of how *normal* he looked, how healthy.

"He doesn't *look* like he had a drug problem," she remarked to Miss Dixie.

Not that she knew what a drug problem looked like. All she really had to go on were movies and episodes of "Intervention." She imagined that his eyes might be bloodshot and glassy, his skin ashy, his hair limp due to infrequent washings and a neglect of hygiene.

Instead, what she was seeing in the multiple social media groups dedicated to the fallen singer was a youthful man with clear blue eyes, glossy brunette locks that fell to his shoulders by the time period's popular style, an easy smile, and skin tanned from the southern California sun.

She flipped through what felt like hundreds of photographs of him relaxing in the California desert with the rest of the band, goofing off as he scampered over boulders with the energy of a young kid and posing on his motorcycle.

"He loved the desert so much," Ruby had shared with her on a visit. "He said it was the one place where he felt like he could find God. Parker wasn't a religious man, but he was a spiritual one. He loved going out there alone, lying on the hood of his car, and watching the stars. Said they were brighter out there."

Taryn now had an aching desire to visit Parker's desert.

She found shots of him leaning back against a shabby old couch in an undisclosed living room, surrounded by laughing friends, a beat-up guitar lovingly balanced on his knees.

Standing on a dusky stage, eyes closed and head tilted back, a glaring spotlight focused on him. His Nudie Suit with its marijuana leaves, rolling dice, and ruby red lips set afire by the beams of light, making him appear to glow.

Never did he look better or happier, however, than when he was with Ruby. As with their music, the two of them sharing a frame was nothing short of magic.

The carefree, girlish figure who stood with her arms wrapped around his waist and her head on his shoulder was a far cry from the sophisticated, soft-spoken woman who'd played for royalty and was revered for her charity work.

The girl who had waved her tambourine as she danced around Parker on the stage, posed with her tongue stuck out next to Parker in front of a now-demolished Vegas hotel, and stood on the bed of a truck with a beer in her hand and the sun setting behind her was gone. Part of her had probably died in that motel room alongside him. (Though Taryn *had* seen a glimpse of her on the patio, the puppies cavorting at her feet.)

It was for that girl and boy that Taryn was going to see this through to the bitter end for. They deserved it. Ruby deserved some peace. If Taryn could give it to her, then she couldn't *not* finish what she'd started.

She couldn't disappoint Ruby, Miss Dixie, or herself. Taryn just wasn't built that way.

AKER *STOOD* back, arms crossed over chest, and considered the canvas as Taryn lugged it from the trunk of her car. When he let out a slow, loud whistle Taryn stopped and turned. "What's wrong?" she asked.

"What made you go with *that*?"

"Huh?" Taryn put the painting down and gently leaned it against the wheel. She then walked over to Aker and stood next to him. Together, they looked at the painting.

She had been staring at it almost nonstop for the past eight days but now she tried to step out of her own head and examine it through Aker's eyes. His poker-face was impossible to read, but his eyes were burning. She thought she might know why.

"It's the wall isn't it?" she asked.

Aker nodded.

The painting presented the past. The furnishings and décor were straight out of the late 1960s and what would have filled the room when Parker and the rest of the band had stayed there. She hadn't conveyed anything modern into the artwork at all.

"So what is *that*?"

"I don't know," Taryn replied honestly.

And she didn't. She'd watched those shadows prance across the wall for a week. For nearly eight days she'd watched as it started near the floor and slowly reached upwards, until it met the ceiling and began spreading towards the middle of the room, stretching to her. It was only recently that she realized the shadow was growing, *expanding*, because it was signaling a person entering the room. It grew larger as the figure drew closer.

That shadow was as much a part of the room's past, and Taryn's *present*, as the mirror. She couldn't leave it out.

"I think it's important," she added. She hadn't meant for Aker, or anyone, to see the painting before it was finished. Now that she'd seen his reaction to it, she was even more uncertain of her decision to include it.

Aker nodded but didn't look convinced.

Taryn turned and looked at him. "I think it has to do with Parker," she said, watching his face for a sign of life.

He wouldn't meet her probing gaze.

"Parker was *alone* that night," Aker barked. He straightened his shoulders, turned, and brusquely stomped to his chair where he busied himself unfolding a blanket and straightening it over the seat, readying it for his long wait.

It was Taryn's turn to be skeptical. "Are you *sure*?"

Everything she'd read, seen, and felt shouted that Aker had been with Parker that last night, either before or after his death. Whether that implicated him in the singer's demise was questionable but she was certain he'd been dishonest regarding his whereabouts that evening. It was a feeling as much as it was a combination of the interviews and information both she and Matt had read following the death.

"Parker was *alone*," Aker repeated, keeping his back to her. "If someone had been there he wouldn't have died the way he did. He would've gotten help. It wouldn't have been too late."

"Maybe they were scared. Maybe they thought they'd get in trouble," Taryn said. "Police didn't find any drugs in the room, only in his system. Shouldn't there have been some there with him? Something? Maybe someone thought they were protecting him and took them away before anyone could get there."

"And *maybe* the authorities aren't as clean as some people think," Aker snorted. "That was a different time. I quit for a reason."

"And you went back," Taryn pointed out.

Aker didn't reply and continued his stony stance.

"Why wasn't he with Ruby?" Taryn could be like a dog with a bone, and she had lots of questions she wanted answers to. Aker was the only one who could answer them at the moment. She wasn't ready to go to her employer. "Ruby was just down the road. Why wasn't he with *her*, staying with her, being with her?"

Aker turned at that, his face paling. "Leave Ruby out of this," he snapped. Taryn thought she might have seen his lips quiver a little, but she knew she *must* be seeing things. "If she'd known some of the things that were going on she would've..."

"Would've what?"

Aker's shoulders slumped in defeat. He suddenly looked much older and less powerful. "She was always a smart girl. Not just pretty, but so smart. She was better than that, always better than those around her. She should've hightailed it out of there long before things for the way they did. They think they can save the world. They think they can save everyone. Some people just aren't worth saving. Some *can't* be. People like that, like *you*, they don't know when to stop."

"Like *me*?"

"That's what you're doing here, right?" Aker gestured with his hands, taking in the parking lot and building. "Here. Trying to bring back the past so that you can fix it? I see what you're doing and, more importantly, I see what it's doing to *you*. You think I don't notice? I saw it in her, too. It took over her life. Took over his, too, if you want to be honest about it. Don't let it take over yours."

Taryn was stunned into silence. Feeling vaguely embarrassed and ashamed, she looked down at her feet. They'd suddenly become very interesting. Her toes were cold in the Birkenstocks but she'd appreciate having them once she entered the room.

"I know more than you think," he said.

Taking one last look at the painting before averting his eyes and slipping on his sunglasses, he shook his head. "Don't you have work to do?"

Taryn kept to herself as she carried her supplies across the parking lot to the motel room. Aker stayed seated and flipped through his book.

It was only after she was inside with her jacket removed and her hair pulled back off her neck in a ponytail that she realized the other thing troubling her: Aker hadn't checked the perimeter or any of the rooms. It was the first time he'd let her go in first.

TWENTY-SIX

She'd been working on the painting for over a week; Taryn should've been finished but she wasn't. She'd done nothing but work on it, rarely stopping long enough to eat or grocery shop or even sleep for more than a few hours at a time. She'd taken to sleeping in the evenings as soon as she got home, waking up around midnight so that she could work through the night.

The nightmares weren't as bad when she slept in the evening.

Taryn had put so much work into the painting of Room #5–details that only she would ever see. The wood grain was so lifelike that she feared getting splinters if she ran her fingers over the nightstand. The radiance of the sunlight streaming in through the tiny window was warm to the touch; the heat that wafted from the radiator thawed her fingers when her own heater in her apartment failed.

The shadow that loomed over the room, stretching up the wall and reaching towards the center of the ceiling, observed all that went on, a witness to the secrets and actions of that night.

She thought it might be one of her best pieces of work.

But she couldn't finish it.

"You have to let me go Parker," she rasped, her throat sore and scratchy. "I have other things to do here. You have to let me out of this room."

The equine painting was back; the horse was running across the field now, his mane flying straight back from his glorious head. The barn had vanished. She yearned for the wind she could almost feel from the painting.

"Remember," the soft voice whispered from the bed, tempting her to come closer.

The pain in Taryn's hip and legs throbbed. Her heart pounded in her chest as her blood bubbled under her skin. The pressure in her head was so intense she thought her brain might be expanding.

She did not feel well.

Most of all, though, was the desperation she felt inside. The hopelessness was overwhelming. She'd tried to take a walk around her block the night before. It was a pleasant evening and the children playing outside had warmed her soul. It was still daylight when she got home and, rather than staying cooped up inside and watching it grow dark, she'd been excited at the prospect of getting out and walking around.

She'd barely gotten to the bottom of her stairs when the pain in her legs had grown so intense that she'd burst into embarrassing tears—even more embarrassing because two of her perky neighbors were coming in the front door at the same time and had seen her. They were both Vanderbilt graduate students, both in their early twenties, and still had the bubbly personalities and perfect figures that only college co-eds seemed to be able to possess.

They'd offered to help her back up but Taryn had declined. She'd rather crawl.

She'd literally had to hold onto the railing and pull herself up the stairs, one step at a time. When she'd finally fallen through her door, she'd vomited right there by the basket where she kept her umbrellas. It had been a nice soup, too—one of those expensive, creamy ones with real chunky vegetables.

She didn't think she'd ever be able to eat that soup again and that was too bad since she'd bought eight cans of it.

Until the sun set, Taryn had sat at her window, looking out over the expansive lawn in front of the building. Children kicked a ball back and forth to each other as hip and energetic parents stood on the side and cheered them on. Pedestrians crossed against a light, rushing to the other side of the street with their hair flying out behind them, bakery bags in one hand and a steaming cup of coffee in another. Bikers and joggers whizzed by on the sidewalk.

Taryn wasn't a part of any of it. She might as well have been watching it all through a television screen. Life was going on around her and it didn't feel like she was ever going to be a part of it at all.

Now, sweating and steaming in the motel room, she thought about Parker on that last night.

Had he felt that same way? Had he been ready to throw in the towel? What had happened between him and Ruby? They'd loved each other, that was obvious through their songwriting and numerous photographs. The looks they'd shared between them, the touches depicted in the candid shots...the lyrics she'd continued to pen about him long after his death.

Matt loved her too, of course. Maybe it wasn't fair to think that Ruby could've saved Parker. When you were that deep inside yourself, that lost, it was hard to feel the light anymore. Sometimes you even thought you didn't deserve it.

Cruel laughter filled the room, a harsh sound that stuck to Taryn and drilled deep into her skin. It was a mean sound, full of ridicule.

Was it male? Female? She couldn't tell.

Taryn covered her ears with both hands and shook her head from side to side, trying to get it to go away.

"Mind over matter, mind over matter," she chanted.

The laughter continued, growing louder by the second.

Taryn dropped to the bed in front of her and crawled to the middle. The bed was clean now, still covered in a generic motel room floral blanket, but not home to the urine and excrement it usually boasted. Taryn curled up in the middle and brought her knees to her chest.

Keeping her hands still on her ears she found comfort in the fetal position and tried to imagine cuddling close to Matt, to her grandmother, to Andrew.

Was it too late to call out for her mommy?

"Mommy," she whimpered, scared and ashamed. When the fear became so strong, it was primal to call out to a mother, even when that mother was a symbolic one. Taryn's had certainly never been comforting.

The room began shaking then, tremors that vibrated the bed and pained her.

"Parker, stop!"

Though the incessant laughing and shaking continued, something crawled up behind her and molded its body to hers. She could feel the heat of the figure next to her,

299

feel the hardness of a thigh and legs as they molded themselves to hers. The desperation permeated strongly from behind her, but there was comfort in the companionship and, together, they held on through the heat and insanity.

Suddenly, the room's front door flew open. A gust of cold air washed over Taryn, knocking the breath out of her. The lamps flickered once then went dead, leaving the room in shadows again. The bedspread under her sent waves of acrid filth drifting upwards, making Taryn gag. The equine painting was once again replaced.

Aker stood before her, nothing short of horror on his face.

In one swift movement he had his coat off and draped over her then had her up in his arms. He was carrying her out the door before she could speak.

"What are you doing," she asked.

"You're freezing," he said shortly, marching towards his car.

"I'm burning up," she insisted. "I'm sweating."

"That room is an ice chest," he barked. "It gets colder by the day. I'd say it's not a degree over forty in there right now."

Taryn couldn't believe it. She'd been so hot.

"Has it been like that every day this week?" she asked weakly.

"Yes, every day. Each day you come out of there, looking like death. Your skin's been turning blue."

"I didn't know. I felt hot..."

"You need to stay out of there," he said. "Here, get in my car."

Taryn waited as he turned up the heat and turned on his seat warmers. "Just move those over," he barked, gesturing at the pile of photographs that littered his seat.

Taryn obliged and began picking them up, one by one, so as not to crush them.

"I'll be right back. Just put them in the back.

She held the photos in her hand and waited as he turned and went back to the room. He emerged carrying her painting supplies and canvas. These, he placed in his trunk.

Taryn was about to put the stack of 4X6 photos in the backseat, when one caught her eye. The man in the picture was much younger, and had a full head of hair, but it was definitely Aker. He stood next to a smiling Parker, whose arm was slung around a laughing Ruby, Lenny, and a woman. The woman next to Aker, the one with the pouty lips and full bosom, had to be the same one Taryn had seen in bed with Parker.

"Hey Aker," Taryn asked when he slid back inside the car. "Who is this?"

She pointed to the picture of the group.

Aker frowned. "That's my ex-wife, Gloria. Ruby asked for these photos. I can't imagine why."

Taryn nodded silently and gently placed them in the back.

"I'll have someone come back and get your car later," he said as they pulled out of the parking lot. "You need to get home, get warm, and get some rest."

Taryn nodded, still stunned.

"And, frankly, a bath wouldn't hurt."

"DID *YOU* hear what I said, Taryn?"

Matt's voice sounded a thousand miles away, though, and Taryn was struggling to concentrate on it. She'd slept for hours and woke up disoriented, confused by the sound of her telephone. Now she sat in the darkness of her living room, trying to remember what day it was.

"I'm sorry, what?"

"Taryn," Matt's voice was filled with concern. "Are you sure you're okay?"

"I'm just tired," she replied, but it was so much more than that. She felt like she was falling apart.

"Did you hear what I said about the review, the one on your portfolio website?"

"Uh huh," she said. "Yeah."

But she hadn't.

"No you didn't," Matt said, reading her mind. "If you'd heard me then you would've reacted more strongly."

"I'm sorry, Matt." Taryn rubbed at her temples and slumped back on her couch. The familiarity of her apartment was soothing but her skin still prickled with a harsh reminder of the fear and peculiarity that had overcome her earlier that day in the motel room.

"The review, the bad one?"

"Yes." She was listening now, and focusing on his words.

"It came from right there in Nashville," Matt told her. "There wasn't a name attached to it but Rob traced the IP address to a computer in Nashville."

Taryn straightened now, her blood running a little cold. "From here? Well that's weird. Maybe I pissed off a neighbor or something."

"Yeah, well, I'd be careful if I were you," Matt cautioned her. "You seem to have made someone mad, and that someone is close enough to you that it has me worried."

"It's just an online bully," Taryn said lightly, trying her best to shrug it off. "I can handle one of those."

She wasn't so sure, though. She didn't get out much and see anyone regularly enough to make them mad. She hadn't seen her high school classmates since graduation. Her college friends had all moved on, most out of the city altogether.

She'd obviously upset someone, though, and pretty well at that. Maybe it was time to start watching her back.

TWENTY☐SEVEN

I'*m worried about you, honey,*" Ruby said.

Taryn was embarrassed that Ruby was sitting in her disorganized apartment across from her but Ruby looked as comfortable as she did anywhere else.

Still feeling a little rough and out of sorts, Taryn stayed inclined on the sofa. She brought her Sherpa throw up under her chin and clutched it tightly. "I have to finish the paintings," she said, trying not to let the panic show in her voice.

"Sweetie, they're not that important. I shouldn't have asked you to do them. I've heard stories about that motel for years. I knew what you were walking into," Ruby moaned, shaking her head. "This is my fault."

"No, I want to help you. If I stop this now…"

It will be like admitting defeat. This is my purpose now, Taryn thought, seeing these to the end. I can't quit.

"Aker said the room was unreasonably cold," Ruby said.

"It felt warm to me."

"He said you could see things that weren't there, like the bedding."

"I'm not crazy," Taryn muttered, although now she was wondering if she might be headed that way.

"Of course not," Ruby said soothingly, patting her on the foot. "But you're sensitive and I knew that and sent you in anyway. Maybe you just need a break."

Taryn rolled over on her side and raised up on her elbow. "Ruby, did Aker tell you that I needed to quit?"

"He suggested it," Ruby replied. "He's just worried about you."

"Hmmm...Let me ask you something else. Are you positive Aker wasn't there that night Parker died? Or that Parker was even alone?"

Ruby looked down at her long fingers and picked an invisible piece of lint from them. "I don't think Aker was there. I think Parker was by himself."

She's hiding something, Taryn thought. *I know it.*

Ruby's phone rang then, saving both women from any further probing. Taryn listened as the color drained from Ruby's face.

"Is it okay? Is everything still there?"

There was a pause and Taryn watched Ruby's face fall. "Oh dammit. Are you sure? And outside too?"

Taryn sat up and wrapped the blanket around her. "Is everything okay?" she mouthed.

"Black Raven Inn," Ruby mouthed back.

Taryn felt herself deflate. Did something happen? Was it still there?

Ruby's end consisted of a few more questions and then she hung up, her shoulders limp and her face pained.

"Someone broke into the hotel, into Parker's room," she explained. "They trashed it. Trashed the little monument outside as well. Aker thinks it was just some kids trying to make some sort of statement."

"Oh no," Taryn moaned, thinking of all the posters and picture that had been left in his honor. "That's horrible."

Then she thought of her painting. She'd left the canvas in the room when Aker had taken her to his car. At least he'd gone back for it, at least he'd saved it.

"I'm sorry Ruby," she said sympathetically.

Ruby nodded dully. "Maybe everyone was right. Maybe I'm just a stupid old woman. I just thought that if...I thought that maybe I'd see him. Maybe I could finally say goodbye. Maybe I'd finally have a doorway to him."

So that was it, Taryn thought. *Ruby wasn't looking for a final goodbye–she was looking to be with him again, however she could get him.*

Oh, but if she knew the kind of angry state Parker was in now, she wouldn't want to be with him. He needed to make the transition into the next world, not wait around and be tied to this one.

Taryn was struck with her own revelation. Andrew was gone. She'd never see him again. He wasn't going to come back and haunt her. She'd been disappointed that Miss Dixie had never picked up on him, never revealed him to her.

If she were completely honest with herself, she'd admit that she continued to work with the spirits because it was proof of an afterlife, proof that Andrew still existed somewhere and might come back to her.

She no longer wanted him to return to her. She was happy she'd never seen him. She hoped that, wherever he was, he was at peace. Not like Parker. That was far worse than never seeing him again.

Some things were worse than death.

WITH *A* renewed vigor, Taryn marched around her apartment and picked up stray pieces of clothing and garbage. She'd already done two loads of laundry and was getting ready to do a third. She had clean towels for the first time in weeks. She also had clean dishes and had been able to eat a whole turkey sandwich and cup of tomato soup.

Proud of herself, Taryn even sang a little tune as she walked around. She hurt and was still depressed but there was a light at the end of the tunnel.

She was almost sure it wasn't a freight train.

When Matt called, she was downright cheerful.

"Taryn, I think you need to stay away from Aker," he said, stopping her in her tracks.

"What?"

"The bodyguard," he said. "I got your email about the break in. Think about it, though. You said you were sweating every day and yet he said the room was freezing? What if he was just messing with you? What if he was going in every day and turning on the heat and then tried to convince you that you were crazy?"

Taryn set the clothes basket down and landed on the floor next to it, stunned.

"The hell you say!"

"And you said he got upset at the painting with the shadow?"

"Yeah..."

"What if he got upset because it's his shadow? Now he's trying to talk this Ruby out of keeping you on because he knows you're close to the truth. Think about it, he has complete access to everything you do there."

Taryn felt the beginning of nausea threaten to overtake her. How could she have been so stupid?

"Oh God, Matt, I think you're right," she moaned. "Do you think he...do you think he knows something about Parker? Do you think he's responsible for his death?"

"I think he saw a window of opportunity," Matt said. "I think he showed up as Parker was dying and then left, when he should have gotten help."

"Yeah, but why? What's the motive?"

"Jealousy. You said Parker had a thing with his ex-wife. What if Aker was also in love with Ruby? Makes sense. He's been working as her guard for all these years. His ex-wife goes to Parker, the woman he's obsessed with loves Parker..."

Taryn rubbed at her temple. "But he's had his chance all these years. Why not make a move on her?"

"Maybe he tried," Matt replied. "Maybe she rejected him."

"Then why continue to work with her, to be that close?"

Matt hesitated and then answered, "Because for some men it's enough just to be close to the woman they love, even if the woman doesn't love them back."

He'd waited for her. He'd waited all night. Where was she?

It was tonight. He felt good, he was straight. That night in Tucson had been an eye-opener, the sweetest night he'd ever had. He'd wanted more but she'd held out her hand and gently pushed him back. He'd respected that.

Tonight, though, tonight he would tell her.

This was the beginning. This was just the start.

He hadn't been that giddy since he was a little boy.

When he heard the footsteps outside the door he straightened and ran his hands through his hair. He could hear her hand on the knob, turning it.

Damn it, *he'd locked the door.*

The three feet between the bed and the lock was an eternity. He just wanted her to be there.

He fumbled with the lock for a moment but then it was open and the cool air was rushing in, washing over him. She was in his arms, then, on him before he could catch his breath. Something clinked, a noise that sounded very far away.

The ring, *he thought.* The ring fell.

He closed his eyes.

TWENTY-EIGHT

Matt," *Taryn's voice flew out in a rush* as she ran down the stairs. "I figured it out. It's in the room! It makes total sense now! I've got to get back to the motel room. Call me!"

It was unusual for Matt's phone to go to voicemail but she knew he'd get the message soon and call her right back.

Taryn was as excited as Parker had been in her dream. She'd been wrong. She'd been wrong about a lot. It had all been *right* there in front of her and she'd ignored the signs, ignored what he was trying to tell her.

The ghost wasn't trying to hurt her, he was trying to *show* her. And she'd been blind.

At 1:00 am the roads were clear. She considered calling Matt again to tell him what was going on but decided against it. She didn't want to wake him. She could wait until she found what she was looking for and had proof.

As she neared the motel, though, she changed her mind. She should let him know.

Taryn pulled over to a deserted gas station and quickly tapped out a text message to Matt, telling him where she was and what was going on. Then she laid her phone on her seat and headed back out to the main road. Now at least she could say she tried.

The motel looked much different in the dark of night. The gate was locked and Aker had the key with him. Taryn already knew how to get in, though, and after pulling her car into a nearby fast food lot she slipped back over to the Black Raven Inn and walked around the perimeter until she found the loose opening in the gate. It only took her a few seconds to get inside.

Her little backpack was slung over her shoulder, Miss Dixie fitted snugly inside.

Taryn was across the parking lot and all the way to Room #5 before she remembered her phone.

"Well, damn," she muttered.

For a moment she paused, wondering if she should go back for it. She'd left it on her car seat, forgetting that she'd removed it from her backpack to send a text message to Ruby.

In the end, however, she decided she didn't need it. She wasn't going to be there long and she had her mace. Nobody would bother her. It had already been vandalized the night before. They didn't usually come back if they were unable to find something the first time.

She didn't need a key to Parker's room; the door had been kicked open by the vandal and now it couldn't shut all the way to. Taryn gave it a little push and was soon inside.

She was shocked and saddened at the shape of the room. The bed had been sliced down the middle, stuffing and springs popping out everywhere. The bedspread was in tatters, slimy streamers that had been tossed all over the room. All of Parker's pictures had been torn from the walls, destroyed. It appeared one had been defecated and urinated on.

It didn't look animal.

The chair was overturned and someone had taken a knife to the fabric, ripping it to shreds.

Her easel was broken in half, her paints opened and the contents smeared over the walls and ceiling. Blood-red paint dripped from the ceiling and ran down the walls.

The whole thing looked like a murder scene. This hadn't been the work of some teenagers looking for a good time; this had been done by someone full of anger.

The one thing Taryn needed hadn't been touched.

Not bothering to close the door behind her, she kneeled down at the radiator and, using the screwdriver she'd brought from home, began working on the screws. It was old and the metal was sticking in place, but the top came off soon enough.

Taryn now wished she had her phone with her. At least, if she did, she could've used the flashlight on it. It was pitch black inside it now and she couldn't see what she was sticking her hand into. She just hoped it wasn't a rat's nest or spider nest. She didn't do spiders.

She was about to give up when her fingers hit the round metal object.

Murmuring with glee, Taryn brought her hand back out, the ring clutched between her fingers. It glowed in the moonlight with a preternatural radiance.

The year after Parker died, the heating system had been updated. The old radiator had never been removed. It was her luck the ring was still there.

Taryn knew she needed to get out of there. It was still an unsafe part of town, especially at night. As she turned to go, however, something tugged at her. It might have been

Parker, or it might have been her own subconscious. Either way, she took a few moments to fish Miss Dixie out of her backpack and turn her on. Taryn aimed her at the room in general and then at the bed. When she brought the camera back and gazed at the LCD screen, she was happy with what she saw.

She was in the process of slinging the camera around her neck when she was pushed from behind, a force so great that she slammed into the floor and immediately saw stars. She heard, rather than felt, the crack of her neck. She landed on Miss Dixie as she fell and a rib dislocated from her position. Taryn screamed from the pain then felt a kick in the lower back for her efforts.

When she was flipped over and the pillow was thrown over her face, she began to fight.

TWENTY-NINE

The *world was growing black around her.* Taryn had never seen such darkness.

The panic at being unable to breathe consumed her, had her kicking and thrashing and screaming a pitiful sound that was muffled against the fabric.

But then something else happened.

She was in the room, but she wasn't. Taryn could feel herself being lifted into the air, floating to the ceiling, where she tucked herself into a little ball in the corner. The feeling of weightlessness, of flying, was exhilarating. Her body had never felt so alive, or so pain free. She experimented by doing a little somersault, feeling the world spinning around her. Her face broke out into a wide smile as she laughed and laughed.

The scene before her caught her attention, however, and she stopped.

It was Parker and he was alone. Back and forth he paced across the room, hands running through his hair and tugging, pulling out strands by the clumps. His face pale, his body dripping with sweat, he looked fluish. Taryn's heart went out to the man who was obviously sick, clearly unwell.

She watched with sympathy as he stopped walking, bent over at the waist, and gagged. Then she watched when he fell onto the bed and clutched his stomach, moaning in agony. He was back up again soon after, again pacing back and forth, alternating between crying and cursing.

A knock on the door came then and someone she couldn't see handed something to Parker. When he reentered the room he had a bottle in his hands. He placed the bottle on the nightstand then returned to his pacing, shaking his head back and forth, as though fighting something inside.

Finally, he rushed to the small table, opened the bottle, and removed first one pill and then another. He swallowed them dry then turned to face the wall. She watched as he beat his hands on it and cried out, defeated and repulsed. Minutes later when he turned around, however, the agony on his face had been replaced with something akin to peace. He didn't appear to be high, not in the way Taryn knew. He looked clear, put together. His movements were more fluid, the desperation no longer as obvious.

When he sat back down on the edge of the bed, she thought he even looked normal.

But she'd never seen someone more miserable.

MISS *DIXIE* was crushing into her; she was aware of her camera more than anything else.

For a moment she'd wanted to somersault into the air again. An opening had appeared in the motel's ceiling and roof and she could see the black, starry night above her. Something tugged at her, called her upwards. Taryn had thought about extending her body and just flying up and out, soaring into the cool sky and feeling the weightlessness forever.

It was so much better.

But then she felt Miss Dixie.

She was back on the floor again, the camera digging into her stomach. She could no longer breathe, no longer move.

She could feel her camera, though, and with the last bit of strength she had, she grabbed ahold of the body, tugged it free of its strap (a movement that would leave her neck bruised and scarred for months), and grasped it. Then, with a primal cry, she flailed blindly and struck the figure atop of her with all her might.

The pressure on her face lessened and she could move.

Taryn used the opportunity to roll out from under the pillow. When she saw the outline of the person kneeling before her, clutching their head, she stood and brought Miss Dixie down with all her might. Then she did it again and again, driving her camera into whatever surface on them she could hit.

Satisfied they were still on the floor, Taryn turned to run from the room but was stopped when a hand reached out and grabbed her ankle, dragging her back to the floor. Thinking of Matt, and of Parker, she kicked and fought and screamed a primal sound that rang throughout the motel's complex.

Then her scream was replaced with something else, a blast that sent a spark of fire through the darkness.

The grip on her leg was loosened. Taryn could stand again. The figure was slumped over in front of her, an acrid scent of blood and gunpowder filling the room.

Looking up in surprise, Taryn saw the tall, thin outline of a woman standing in the doorway. Next to her, in a faint silhouette, was Parker Brown. His face, turned to the woman beside him, was as radiant and peaceful as it had been in any photo. Ruby held the gun before her, still and unmoving.

"And this one's for Parker, Lenny," she cooed. And fired again.

THIRTY

Are you sad it's coming down? Just a little?"

Ruby turned and smiled at Taryn. The two women stood side by side as the construction workers milled around the motel's parking lot, shouting and following orders.

"Maybe a little," she replied. "But Parker would want it. He wouldn't want this to be his tomb."

"Well, at least you're making this side of town happy," Taryn teased her and laughed.

The pain rippled through her stomach and chest, a reminder of the events that had occurred a month earlier.

"I don't know whether to be amused or disappointed that the tabloids didn't take a greater interest in what happened," Ruby mused thoughtfully. "I guess nobody's interested in an old woman like me."

"Want me to leak a story or something?" Matt asked, throwing his arm around Taryn. "I could say you were having an affair with Garth Brooks or something."

"Good job, Matt, you know who Garth is."

"Yeah, well, I'm learning," he shrugged.

"Make it Rodney Crowell and you're on," Ruby teased him.

Although he might not have known who Ruby was initially, anyone who would shoot somebody to save Taryn was okay in his book. While she recovered in the hospital, he'd formed an odd sort of friendship with Ruby, even being invited to stay with her until Taryn was released.

Taryn again thought of the night's events. Remembered seeing Ruby in the doorway with the gun, feeling Lenny's hands holding the pillow over her head.

She guessed if you were going to be murdered, there were worse ways you could go than death-by-superstar.

"So the 'girlfriend' who was with Parker earlier that night was Aker's ex wife?" Matt had trouble putting the story together when he'd visited Taryn in the hospital.

"Apparently everyone was sleeping with her, even Lenny," Taryn had laughed wryly, although laughing hurt so she'd quickly nipped that one in the bud.

"And the night he died?"

"Lenny had found out she was sleeping with Parker, too. She knew he was angry. She'd gone there to warn him but it was too late." Taryn sighed, feeling the weight of the world on her shoulders. "Gloria was just a replacement for Ruby, someone Lenny couldn't have. Every time he fell for a woman, she wanted Parker."

She was grateful Matt had called Ruby that night. Even more grateful she'd forwarded that first email to him, the one with Ruby's phone number. If he hadn't called her and told her where Taryn had gone...

Of course, how could she have known that Lenny was stalking her? That's he'd been looking to destroy her paintings and pictures.

That someone that famous had been so crazy?

"Okay ladies," Aker called, marching towards them. "Enough standing around here. Let's get some food."

Taryn smiled as the bulky man threaded his arm through Ruby's and led her to the car. She wasn't sure when that had happened, but it was nice.

In the hospital, Ruby had visited Taryn and asked her what she really wanted to know.

"He didn't overdose, did he?"

Taryn, feeling the effects of the pain medicine, had told her the truth.

"In a way, he did. It wasn't that he'd taken too much, it was that he'd been clean up until that point and had re-dosed at his old dosage. His body just couldn't handle it. If he hadn't been trying to get clean, it might have been okay."

"But he didn't do it."

"No," Taryn said sadly, "he didn't. It was Lenny. Lenny gave him the sedative then shot him up. Parker never knew."

She had the pictures to prove it, too. Miss Dixie had come through in more ways than one.

The ring, which Taryn had clutched until the paramedics had rushed her off, had fallen into the radiator when Lenny entered the room and grasped Parker in a hug. He'd done his best to find it, but couldn't. When he'd heard about Taryn's paintings, he knew she'd figure it out.

"Why was the ring so important?" Matt had asked.

"Because Parker had bought it for him the day before. And he'd told everyone that he hadn't seen Parker since, hadn't been in the motel room. That put him on the scene," she told him.

Then it was Taryn's turn to ask Ruby.

"You and Parker never, you know, did you?"

Ruby shook her head sadly. "No. Just a kiss, one night in Arizona. It was going that way. It would have gone that way. I was going to tell him. I was going to go there and tell him I loved him. But I chickened out. I thought there was so much time. We had that tour coming up, we were talking about a new album. I didn't want to do it over the phone and I didn't feel well that night. I waited."

"So he never knew."

"He never knew," she agreed.

But Taryn thought he had. She thought the idea of Ruby was what held him together.

Later, while talking to Matt, she told him of the things she'd learned. "Parker wasn't an addict in the sense we think of," she said. "He wasn't taking stuff to get high, he was taking things to feel normal, to maintain. There was something in him that just wouldn't give him any peace."

"I hope he has it now," Matt said.

"Me too."

"Listen, do you think all of that was just Parker? The hauntings, the stuff going on in the room?"

Taryn had wondered that herself. "I don't know," she replied at last. "I want to say no. I think there was something else going on. Sometimes darkness follows grief, desperation, lost people. I think at one time it might have just been a normal motel but then over the years it became something else. I know I feel better now that I'm out of it."

"I'm glad it's coming down," Matt had shuddered.

"So am I."

"And maybe now Ruby can find some peace as well. Never underestimate the power of unrequited love. Or guilt. Ruby had both. I hope she can move on now."

Matt laughed as he ruffled Taryn's hair.

"What?"

"Did you hear yourself? 'Move on'," he grinned. "Are you moving to the dark side?"

Taryn bit her lip and tried to hide a smile. "I hope not," she replied.

I hope not.

SPECIAL NOTES

There is a lot of truth in the novel you just finished, although the "true" parts have been lavishly embellished. I am going to attempt to separate truth from fiction now, to give you an idea of the things I completely made up, the things I exaggerated, and the things I didn't change at all.

Firstly, Taryn's love of music is my own. I wrote myself into this book more than any other piece of fiction I've released. Like Taryn, I am a strong music lover. I was able to write about Nashville in such a way because, as a teenager, I moved to Music City and attended Belmont College where I majored in Music Business. I wanted to be a country music singer. Alas, it didn't happen.

The part at the beginning about Taryn and the concept album and 8-track? That's actually true. I made up the Ruby Jane artist, as well as the Civil War album, but the story itself is true. When I was a kid I had a Don Williams 8-track. I played it every single day, up until I was about 5 and it mysteriously vanished from the car...

Taryn's grandmother, Stella, is loosely based on my own grandmother. They share a lot in common. If you REALLY want to read a character that's more faithful to my own grandmother, then check out my Kentucky Witches series. Liza Jane's grandmother is very similar to mine-more so than Stella.

The Black Raven Inn is a conglomeration of several places. It's no *one* motel, thank goodness. I actually got on Trip Advisor's site and pulled up some of the motels with the worst reviews and drew inspiration from them. A lot of the Black Raven Inn's descriptions came from these motels.

While backpacking Croatia in my early twenties, I spent the night at a youth hostel in the capital city of Zagreb. It was, by far, the worst hostel I've ever stayed in. Going by the reviews, others agreed. I drew from my experience with that hostel to help flesh out the motel in the book.

Some people will see similarities to the Drake Motel in downtown Nashville and the Joshua Tree Inn and Motel in Joshua Tree, California. The Drake Motel has been around for many decades and, in the past, was a place that up and coming singers would stay while they tried to find their footing in Nashville. It's a typical motor lodge. It had its heyday many years ago but some people still like to drive past it to take pictures of its sign.

The Joshua Tree Inn and Motel in Joshua Tree is a quaint, vintage motel that my son and I stayed in during the research phase of this book. It's reportedly haunted by the ghost of Gram Parsons and we stayed in the "Gram Parsons'

Room" while were there. We loved our stay. It's clean, cute, has a vintage feel to it, and the staff was awesome. I highly recommend that you check it out if you're around Joshua Tree. Which brings us to...

Parker Brown.

Parker Brown is a mixture of several different people. His personality is entirely made up. His career and death, however, ARE loosely based on those of Gram Parsons. I am a huge fan of his, to the point where my son and I visited California to trace some of his steps and sleep in his old hotel room. The shrine outside the room where he overdosed is real.

I really *did* hear guitar music in the middle of the night. If you want to watch a video about our stay there, you can find it on my You Tube channel.

The name "Parker Brown" comes from the fact that my son can never remember Gram Parson's name and, consequently, always refers to him as "Parker."

I combined several different stories of singers' deaths and struggles with addiction to create the idea of "Parker." Lenny is entirely made up. No such person ever existed.

Country music and music in general lost a great talent the day Gram died. He was a beautiful man with a sad, tormented soul. I became very close to his memory as I wrote this book. As a result, I found parts of this book hard to write. I became extremely involved, to the point where I had to put the book down and pick it back up again months later (I wrote *A Broom with a View* in the middle).

The name "Ruby Jane Morgan" comes from two of my aunts–Jane and Ruby. Aunt Jane is responsible for introducing me to a lot of musicians I've come to like as an adult. She gave me an Emmylou duets album when I was a freshman in college and "Gulf Coast Highway," her duet with Willie Nelson, changed my life and the way I viewed music from there on out. My Aunt Ruby always felt more like a sister than an aunt to me. When my Aunt Wilma, a big influence on my life, passed away in the fall of 2015 I knew I needed to do something in honor of the other two relatives who had meant a lot to me over the years. It was Aunt Jane who turned me on to Gram Parsons and Aunt Ruby who, along with grandmother, solidified my love of Elvis. This book is, in part, a tribute to those fine ladies who love music as much as I do.

David and Matt are fictional. People who are close to me will see a resemblance of a childhood friend I grew up with in Matt. He is also equally based on the character of "Spencer Reid" from "Criminal Minds." David is entirely made up and, alas, exists only as a figment of my imagination.

VISIT AMAZON

Did you like what you read? Reviews are very important to authors—leaving a review is like leaving an author a tip!

Visit *Black Raven Inn's* Amazon page at:

http://www.amazon.com/Black-Raven-Inn-Paranormal-Mystery-ebook/dp/B01D284RB4/

ABOUT REBECCA

Rebecca Patrick-Howard is the author of several books including the first book in her paranormal mystery trilogy *Windwood Farm.* She lives in eastern Kentucky with her husband and two children.

Visit her website at www.rebeccaphoward.net and sign up for her newsletter to receive free books, special offers, and news.

WANT MORE TARYN?

Want to learn about Taryn's beloved grandmother and get a glimpse of Taryn when she was a child? The companion novella to the Taryn's Camera series entitled *Stella* is 100+ pages and available in the *Ghost Children* anthology.
For more information visit:

http://www.amazon.com/Haunted-Children-Collection-Stories-Beyond-ebook/dp/B0149ES7J8/

OTHER BOOKS BY REBECCA

Visit Rebecca's website at www.rebeccaphoward.net for ordering information.

Taryn's Camera Series
Windwood Farm

Griffith Tavern

Dark Hollow Road

Shaker Town

Jekyll Island

Taryn's Pictures: Photos from Taryn's Camera

True Hauntings
Haunted Estill County

More Tales from Haunted Estill County

A Summer of Fear

The Maple House

Four Months of Terror

Two Weeks: A True Haunting

Three True Tales of Terror

Other Books
Coping with Grief: The Anti-Guide to Infant Loss

Three Minus Zero

Estill County in Photos

Haunted: Ghost Children Stories from Beyond

REVIEWS FOR
THE
TARYN'S CAMERA
SERIES

Windwood Farm

"This is an absolutely wonderful book and I didn't want to put it down. It was exciting and sad but it was uplifting too." (Kim @ **The Open Book Society** openbooksociety.com/)

"I won't spoil anything but this book has great characterization, loads of atmosphere and is never dull. The first book in the Taryn's Camera series so roll on number two!" (**A Drunken Druid's Reviews** the-drunken-druid.blogspot.com/)

"The author does a great job painting just what life in a small town in Kentucky is like. She also writes a great mystery." (Lisa Binion @ **The News in Books** thenewsinbooks.com/)

"while I do not believe in ghosts and such, this book was written in a way that I was able to enjoy it and go along for the ride and "believe" the story.''- online reviewer

"a great chiller that was perfect summertime reading!''- online reviewer

Griffith Tavern:

"I actually love Rebecca's descriptive style of writing which kept feeding my imagination and continuously created images and pictures in my mind''- online reviewer

"If you like old houses, historic preservation, AND creepy ghost stories, it's right up your (darkened, cobwebby) alley''- online reviewer

"This was a book that was an absolute pleasure to read. A book that I couldn't wait to get back to''- online reviewer

Dark Hollow Road:

"Her characters are rich, her story lines are enticing and as a reader these combine to make for a lovely journey through a small southern town"- online reviewer

"I've enjoyed all of the Taryn's Camera books. They have so many things I love - old houses, ghosts, a likable main character I can relate to, and realistic descriptions of small town Southern life. But this one goes a step further, addressing real life issues with a depth of emotion that can only come from someone who knows this region and its issues firsthand. Highly recommended."- online reviewer

Shaker Town:

"a paranormal whodunit with lots of surprises"- online reviewer

"As always wonderful thorough research was done. Great presentation. I did not want to stop reading until I finished"- online reviewer

"Wonderful story, history, background and my favorite characters! You won't be disappointed with this newest adventure of Taryn and her camera!"- online reviewer

COPYRIGHT

www.ingramcontent.com/pod-product-compliance
Lightning Source LLC
Chambersburg PA
CBHW060125130626
46556CB00006B/2232